Ernestine & Amanda

Ernestine & Amanda

❧ Sandra Belton ❧

SIMON & SCHUSTER BOOKS FOR YOUNG READERS

SIMON & SCHUSTER BOOKS FOR YOUNG READERS
An imprint of Simon & Schuster Children's Publishing Division
1230 Avenue of the Americas, New York, New York 10020

Book design by Heather Wood • The text for this book is set in Goudy Old Style.
Printed and bound in the United States of America
10 9 8 7 6 5 4 3 2   First Edition

Library of Congress Cataloging-in-Publication Data
Belton, Sandra.
Ernestine and Amanda / by Sandra Belton. — 1st ed.
p.   cm.
Summary: Although they do not like each other at first, two girls who take piano lessons
from the same teacher, share friendship with twin sisters, and have their own personal problems
each gradually find their feelings about the other changing.   ISBN 0-689-80848-8
[1. Friendship—Fiction. 2. Family life—Fiction. 3. Afro-Americans—Fiction.] I. Title.
PZ7.B4197Er   1996   [Fic]—dc20   96-11823

Special thanks to Ms. Joellen El-Bashir of the Mooreland-Spingarn Research Center of Howard University,
Washington, D.C., and to Mrs. Argia Watson, Cyndi McClendon, and Terrel Thompson of the Randolph
Magnet School, Chicago, Illinois.

To James Sidney Hammond,
always first!

Ernestine & Amanda

Ernestine & Amanda ♫

"AMANDA?"

"What?"

"You been lookin' through that curtain practically forever. Are you ever gonna give anybody else a chance?"

"I have *not* been standin' here that long, Ernestine."

"You have so."

"Have not."

"Yes, you have, too. But you might as well keep on now. You've already brought yourself bad luck."

"What are you talkin' about?"

"Remember? Miss Elder told us it would be bad luck to look at the audience through the stage curtain before the show starts."

"So how come you're so anxious to look through?"

" 'Cause it's *good* luck to have somebody tell you to 'break a leg' before the show starts, and somebody has already said that to me."

"You think you're gonna have good luck because some-body told you to 'break a leg'? Weird. Really weird."

"Who you callin' weird?"

"I'm not callin' anybody weird. I just said—"

"I heard what you said, Amanda. I've been listenin' to your mouth for months."

"What do you mean, 'months'?"

"Just what I said. Months. You know, like January, February, March…"

"I know what months are, Ernestine. I mean, why are you sayin' you been listening to my mouth for months?"

" 'Cause you always runnin' off at the mouth. You have been ever since that first time I saw you."

"I have not."

"Have so."

"Have not. And anyhow, that first time at Miss Elder's was months and months and months ago, and you probably don't remember back that far any more than I do…"

September

1 ❧ Ernestine

"BYE, MAMA."

I held the handle of the screen door to make sure it wouldn't slam shut. If Mama heard the door, she would say I had slammed it on purpose.

Just my luck. Jazz was sittin' on the porch steps. Other than playing in our big front yard, sitting on the front porch is Jazz's favorite thing to do. I could tell by the look on her face that she had heard everything—while she sat there.

"Whachu lookin' at me for, Jessie Louise?" I stuck my tongue out at her.

My sister hates to be called by her real name. Most of the time she won't even talk to anybody who uses it. That's what I figured she would do then. I figured wrong.

"Wassa matter, Ernestine? Why does the musical gee-nee-us look so sad?"

Jazz had that fake sweet look on her face. The one she

puts on right after church so the huggers won't get mad when she pulls away from them.

"If I'm mad it's because I'm related to someone too dumb to know her real name, which is JESSIE LOUISE."

I practically shouted the words as I walked by Jazz. I figured that would shut her up.

That time I figured right.

I also figured I'd better get away fast just in case Mama heard me yelling at Jazz. I was almost running by the time I bumped into Daddy, who was coming through the front gate.

"Watch out, Ernestine!" Daddy caught hold of me just in time. If he hadn't I would have fallen flat on my face.

"Where you rushin' to?" he asked me. I was bending over to pick up the book and newspaper I had bumped out of his hands.

"I'm not rushin' to no place. I was just gettin' away fast." I handed Daddy his stuff. The newspaper was all messed up. "Sorry, Daddy," I said as he took it.

"So, why are you hurrying with no place to go?" Daddy had on a half-and-half face. A frown on the top half and a smile on the bottom.

Jazz had come to the fence. I knew she'd be butting in, so I started walking and pulling Daddy along.

"Daddy, you gotta help me," I said.

"What's the problem?" Daddy was trying to organize the newspaper sheets.

Jazz was still on the other side of the fence. But she was moving right along with us.

"Come on, Daddy," I said, trying to pull him away from the fence. "I really need to talk to you."

Daddy stopped and looked at me. The frown half on his face went away. "Okay, Buddy. I'll join you on a short walk to no place."

"Buddy" is Daddy's pet name for me. He's the only one who calls me that. He's the only one I *let* call me that. I don't like to be called anything but my name. Ernestine.

"I wanna come, too, Daddy." Jazz was heading for the gate.

My feelings must have jumped to my face, and Daddy must have seen them. "Not this time, Jazz," he said.

Daddy handed his messed-up newspaper to my messed-up sister. "Here, Jazz," he said, "take this in the house for me. And listen out for the phone. I'm expecting a call from Uncle J. B."

Jazz was still standing there as Daddy and I walked away. I wanted to turn around and grin at her, but I decided to leave well enough alone.

We walked down the sidewalk. I took the same size steps as Daddy so our shoes would click on the cement at the same time.

CLOP-tic. CLOP-tic. CLOP-tic.

I could tell Daddy was waitin' for me to say something. So I did. "How was work today?" I asked.

"A normal day," Daddy said. "Nothing unusual or exciting."

CLOP-tic. CLOP-tic. CLOP-tic.

It was getting harder to concentrate. My steps kept getting either ahead or behind. I stopped walking. Then, the words started popping out.

"Daddy, how come I have to start taking music lessons from Miss Elder? Miss Helen plays much better than Miss

Elder. You even said so yourself. And Miss Elder has the worst breath in the world!"

Daddy stopped walking, too. He rubbed his hand across his mouth and cheeks. Then he reached over and put his arm around my shoulders and started walking again.

"Buddy, we all agreed that you would start taking music lessons as soon as school started. Your mother, me, *and* you. And school will be starting day after tomorrow. What made you change your mind?"

"I remember us talking about it. You and Mama said it was the best thing to do. But I *don't* remember agreeing. And, anyhow, even if I did, how come I can't change my mind?"

"Can you tell me *why* you want to change your mind?"

I stopped walking. It was time to look Daddy straight in the face.

"Daddy, pleeeeeease don't make me take lessons from Miss Elder. Please, please, pleeeeease don't."

Daddy started rubbing on his face again. I knew he was thinking. I kept talking.

"Everybody says she has breath like a dragon and that she hits your fingers with a stick when you make a mistake and that her mama sits in a big chair and looks at you when—"

"Whoa!"

Right away my words stopped popping out.

"Listen to me, Buddy, and listen good. I don't know who this 'everybody' is, but I *do* know about Miss Elder."

I could tell from Daddy's voice that my time for explaining had run out.

"And what I know is that Miss Elder is a fine music

teacher. She's the best in town. In fact, she's one of the best piano teachers you might come across in your entire life."

I don't want to come across any music teachers in my entire life.

I figured I'd be in big trouble if Daddy heard what I was thinking, so I kept my thoughts to myself and kept listening.

"And I have confidence that once you and she start working together, you are going to feel the same way I do." Daddy smiled at me. It was a whole-face smile and not one of those half-and-half's.

"And, if I'm not mistaken, your first lesson is today." Daddy pulled out his pocket watch and looked at it. "In about ten minutes, right?"

"Right." I tried to not look in Daddy's face.

"If you don't stop to visit anyone on the way, you'll make it there with a few minutes to spare."

Daddy bent over and kissed the top of my head. "Give it a good try, Buddy," he said.

Daddy waved at me before he turned around to go home. I waved back.

"I'll give it a good try, but her dragon breath will probably disintegrate me and you'll never know that I did." This time I said out loud what I was thinking, but I made sure Daddy was too far away to hear.

2 ✍ Amanda

THE BEST THING about being at Miss Elder's is taking music lessons the same time as my best friend, Alicia Raymond. The worst is having to sit in that boring hall with no windows, waiting and waiting. Either waiting for someone to finish their lessons or for me to have mine. All that waiting really gets on my nerves. Even when I find out things I wouldn't have found out if I hadn't been waiting. Like finding out that Ernestine was going to start taking music lessons.

I recognized her right away. As soon as she came through Miss Elder's door. I even remembered that her name was Ernestine. Ernestine Hawkins, Harless, or something like that.

She looked bigger than she had looked when I had seen her at her church. When she was sitting at the piano down near the pulpit, she didn't look as fat as she looked now.

While she stood there talking to Mrs. Elder, she mostly

kept her head down. But I knew why she was doing that. Did I ever! Mrs. Elder's breath is like old garbage.

Mrs. Elder is Miss Elder's mother. We call her the Warden because she watches everything that goes on. Whenever we come for our lessons, she's sitting in the sunporch room—a room on the side of the house. We have to come through that room to get in the house, and that room leads to a hall that leads to the other rooms in the house. Rooms the Warden doesn't want us to mess up. So we sit in the hall to wait for Miss Elder to call us in for our lessons.

Anybody who starts talking or acting up gets the squint-eye from the Warden. But that's enough to make you shut up. Better the squint-eye than having to go out and sit in the sunporch with her and be almost killed by her atom-bomb breath.

The door between the sunporch room and hall wasn't shut all the way. I couldn't hear too much of what Ernestine said, but the Warden's voice was loud. As usual.

"My daughter tells me you've been playing the piano at Central Street Church since you were just a little thing."

The Central Street Church was where I had seen Ernestine. It's not my church, but I go there with my god-mother Frankie sometimes.

"I hear you play almost entirely by ear. Is that true?"

I get tickled when I hear somebody say "playing by ear." I used to imagine an ear running up and down the keyboard, but I know that's not what it means. One time I asked my father if I played by ear. He said I didn't since I always need music to play anything. Anyhow, I think that playing by music is better than playing by ear.

The Warden kept on talking. "Well," she said, "it's better to know how to read music if you're going to be playing the piano."

I couldn't believe it. The Warden and I felt alike about something!

After the Warden finished asking all her questions, Ernestine came into the hall to wait for her lesson. I think she said something when she came in, but I'm not sure. Since I wasn't sure, I didn't say anything.

She sat down three chairs from where I was sitting. I could tell from looking out the corner of my eye that she was looking the other way. That suited me just fine.

Ernestine just *had* to be stuck up. I had heard a lot of people talk about her. About how well she played the piano. And most of them thought it was wonderful how she could play almost anything by ear.

I took a long look at Ernestine out the corner of my eye. I imagined her fat little ear bouncing on the keyboard. I had to bite on my tongue to keep from laughing.

For the longest time the three of us just sat. The Warden in her high-back chair in the sunporch room and me and Ernestine in the hall. Nobody said anything. Finally, the door to Miss Elder's room opened.

Miss Elder came out into the hall. Alicia and Edna, who I had been waiting for, were behind her. Miss Elder gave me one of her little finger waves and said, "We're finally through, Amanda." Then she went right over to Ernestine.

"Ernestine," she said. "I'm so happy to have you here!"

Miss Elder isn't *anything* like her mother, the Warden. In the first place, she always smells nice when she sits next to you on the piano bench. Like soap made out of flowers. And Miss Elder is nice *all* the time. Not just in front of parents.

Edna and Alicia and I were getting our stuff together so we could leave. "Who's that?" Alicia whispered to me while she put on her sweater.

"I'll tell you outside," I said. I was ready to get out of there. Ernestine had gotten out of her chair and was standing beside Miss Elder. Alicia was looking at them with that look she gets sometimes.

Just about all of us like Miss Elder a lot, but Alicia *loves* her. Alicia acts like she wishes Miss Elder were a member of her family. Like an aunt or something. So, when I saw Alicia standing there watching Miss Elder and Ernestine grinning at each other like they had a secret or something, I knew Alicia was getting jealous.

That wasn't right. Alicia is just about the best student Miss Elder has. It wasn't fair that she should be getting jealous over some new person. Especially somebody who played by ear and couldn't even read music!

I handed Alicia her Hannon book that I had been holding while she put on her jacket. Then I leaned close to her like I was ready to whisper something, but I didn't whisper.

"Hurry up, Alicia Bear," I said. I used one of the super special names we have for each other. "We gotta get home," I said. "I think Daddy's gonna take us to the drive-in tonight."

"Did he say he was?" Alicia started to look happier.

"He said he was going to do something special with us, and after I tell him how good all of us played today, I'm sure that's what he'll do."

When we got to the door, we all turned around to wave to Miss Elder.

"Bye, Miss Elder," we said.

"I hope you're right about the drive in, Amanda," Alicia said.

"Just wait. You'll see," I said and smiled at my always-best friend. Then I looked one more time out the corner of my eye at Miss Play-by-Ear-Fatso Ernestine and kept on out the door.

3 🐾 *Ernestine*

"ERNESTINE! Hurry up!"

Clovis was on the sidewalk in front of my house, but I could hear him all the way in the kitchen. I knew he didn't want to get in trouble for being late the first day of school, but if he didn't stop yellin', I was going to get in trouble.

"Jazz, please tell Clovis I'm comin'." Jazz already had her stuff together and was on her way out the door.

"I can't. I'm goin' the back way so I can meet up with Regina. If I go all the way to the front, I'll be late."

Jazz leaned over to kiss Mama on the cheek. "Bye, Mama," she said in that phony sweet voice.

"Bye, baby," Mama said. "On your way out, just run to the front to tell Clovis your sister is on the way."

"But Mama—"

Mama just looked at Jazz. And I just smiled at Jazz.

As soon as Jazz left, I stood in front of Mama. "Mama," I said, "I don't think I should wear this new dress today."

"Ernestine, it's the dress *you* picked out especially to wear today. The first day of school. Last week you loved it. What made you change your mind?"

The dress had gotten so tight around the middle I could hardly breathe. And the green and yellow plaid made me look like a horse! I began to wish I hadn't eaten all those bologna-and-tomato sandwiches. I had sneaked downstairs to make one every night last week so I'd have something to snack on while I read in bed.

But I wasn't about to tell Mama any of that.

"I'd rather save this dress to wear later. Something more special than the first day of school. Do you mind, Mama?"

"It's up to you, sweetheart," Mama said. She got up from the table to pile our breakfast dishes in the sink.

"Thanks, Mama," I said, rushing upstairs to change.

"And, Ernestine?" I heard Mama calling to me just as I put my foot on the first step.

"More roller skating and bicycle riding and less bologna sandwiches might make you like your dress more," she said. "Now, hurry up. I'll go tell Clovis you're on the way."

Sometimes I think I have a little window outside my brain that only my mama can look through.

I figured Clovis would be wearing something new for the first day of school. And I figured right. Everything he had on from his yellow shirt and tan slacks to the tips of his shiny brown loafers was new. He still wore the same old glasses, but they were polished like crazy, too.

"Hey, Clovis," I said when I came out the door. "You look

real nice. Goin' someplace special?"

"Very funny." Clovis got up from the porch swing, where he had been sitting. "It's about time you got ready. What took you so long?"

"Sorry. I had to change my clothes. But we still got plenty of time."

Clovis hates being late. Even one *second* late. Since he's my best friend, I try hard to be on time whenever we're going someplace together. Even to school, where I don't care if I *ever* get there or not.

Clovis walked down our block so fast, I practically had to run to keep up with him. He slowed down at the corner. I guess he figured he had made up the time he had lost waiting for me.

"Don't you want to know about my music lesson?" I said when we slowed down.

"Yeah. I called you last night to ask about it, but nobody was home.

"We went over to Uncle J. B.'s."

"How was it?"

"Fun. Uncle J. B. showed me and Jazz how—"

"Not your uncle's. Your music lesson."

"I know." I'm always trying to tease Clovis because he's so serious.

"Was goin' there as bad as you thought it was gonna be?"

"No. It wasn't really bad at all."

I knew Clovis was surprised at what I was saying. I was surprised myself to hear those words pop out my mouth. I had been complaining about having to take lessons practically the whole summer.

"And Miss Elder is the best part. She's not at all like your cousin Merry Lou said." I made a face just thinking about that stupid Merry Lou.

"What did she tell you?"

"She said Miss Elder had breath so bad you wanted to faint the whole time you were takin' your lesson and that she hit your fingers with a stick every time you made a mistake."

"I can't believe you listened to Merry Lou! You know she's silly and tells lies." Clovis's face was so frowned up, his two eyebrows were almost touching. Merry Lou is one relative he doesn't like a bit.

"She was right about the dragon breath, though." I put my wrist up to my face so my nose wouldn't remember that smell. The smell of Mrs. Elder's breath. "But the smell belongs to Miss Elder's mother and not her."

"Is Miss Elder a better teacher than Miss Helen?"

Clovis likes Miss Helen a lot. Just like I do. She's been our Sunday school teacher forever. And right after Sunday school before church is—maybe I should say *was*—when Miss Helen and I would sit together at the piano.

I learned to play the piano mostly by listening to and watching Miss Helen play. She would play the songs that we were going to sing in church. Then she would tell me to play along with her or to play some of the songs by myself.

Miss Helen said that's the way she learned to play the piano. By watching and listening to her grandmother. She said her grandmother had played in church for years and years.

Miss Helen is always telling me that I have a lot of talent. That I need to start studying music with a real teacher. Somebody who could teach me things she didn't know. In a way I wanted to do that, too, but mostly I didn't. The biggest part of the "didn't" was not wanting to hurt Miss Helen's feelings. And that's what Clovis's question made me think about.

"I don't know what kind of teacher Miss Elder is yet," I said. "I've only been one time." I knew I was going to like Miss Elder, but I was still having funny feelings about Miss Helen not being my teacher.

Clovis tiptoed around a puddle in the middle of the sidewalk. He was sure being careful not to mess up his new shoes.

"Startin' new with anything is a pain," he said, bending over to check his shoes and make sure no muddy water had splashed on them. "Like startin' out the year in a new room with a new teacher."

"Yeah," I said. I knew that starting to make friends with that snotty bunch of girls who took lessons at Miss Elder's the same time I did was going to be a pain. A real pain. Especially the one Miss Elder called Amanda. Anybody could tell she thought she was cute. But I didn't say anything to Clovis about any of that.

"You know what I hate the most?" Clovis stopped walking.

"What?"

"At the beginning of every year I have to explain over and over that my name is 'Clo-VEESE,' not 'CLO-vis.' I *hate* havin' to do that." Clovis's eyebrows started coming together again.

"So call yourself Bernard. That's your middle name, and it's a hard name to mess up."

"Why should I have to change my name because some teacher is a thick-head?"

"You don't."

Our school was just around the corner. I began to walk faster. I was thinking about some of my friends who I hadn't seen since school let out before summer.

"Don't change your name. Just pretend you're short, green, and grow in a field, *CLO*-vis!"

I took off. I knew Clovis wouldn't even try to catch me. He wasn't about to mess up his first-day-of-school new shoes running across that muddy playground. No way.

4 🖋 *Amanda*

FRIDAY NIGHTS are boring. I like it when Friday finally comes because it means no more school for two whole days, but unless there's something special to do, that night is always boring. A lot of times on Friday night I have to end up in my sister Madelyn's room, waiting for her to do something interesting.

Madelyn was sitting at her dresser, staring in her mirror and brushing her hair. My sister has got to be the vainest person in the universe. If there are people vainer than her, I sure wouldn't want to meet them. I couldn't believe how long she sat there looking at herself and brushing her hair. Probably thinking about that drippy boy. The one she was whispering to Mother about in the kitchen after dinner.

Since I didn't have anything else to do, I decided to say something to help her out. "Madelyn, you're gonna brush all your hair out. Then that drippy boy won't ever look at you."

She stopped looking at herself and looked at me over her shoulder. But her brush didn't miss one lick.

"You should mind your own business, Amanda. Especially since you don't know what you're talkin' about."

I made that humph sound Grandmother Nelson always makes when Madelyn wears her too-tight sweaters. It's a sound that drives Madelyn crazy.

"I do know what I'm talking about. I know you just *loooove* that whoever-he-is."

"You don't know anything."

I must have known something. Madelyn slammed her brush down and got up from the stool she'd been sitting on.

"Don't you have something to do? Something in *your* room?" Madelyn said, flopping down on her bed.

"Nope," I said. Then I stretched across the foot of the bed.

Madelyn did one of her long breaths. The kind she's been doing a lot these days. And not just with me. With Mother and Dad too.

"Amanda," she said. "Why are you trying to bother me?"

"Why do you think I'm trying to bother you? Why can't I just be in here visiting my favorite sister?"

"I'm your *only* sister, Amanda. Your only sibling." Madelyn did another long breath. "Don't give me that mess," she said.

Madelyn rolled over on her side.

"C'mon, Maddie," I said. "Why won't you talk to me?"

"Because, *Mandy,* you don't want to talk. You want to bother me."

I hate being called 'Mandy' the same way Madelyn hates

being called 'Maddie.' It was time for a truce.

"Okay, Madelyn," I said. "If you'll talk to me, I'll try real hard not to bother you."

"What do you want to talk about?" Madelyn said. She was still lying on her side.

"Anything. Like…what's it like being in high school?"

"It's the same way it was last year."

"How was that?"

"Okay, I guess."

"Isn't it better than last year? Don't you know more people now and stuff?"

Madelyn finally turned over. She stretched out and put her hands behind her precious hair.

"Yeah, I do. Lots more people," she said. She was starting to smile. "I think this is going to be a good year."

"Why? Because of that boy?" I tried hard not to sound bothering.

"Are you going to start that again, Amanda?"

I sat up and looked at her. "No, no, I'm not, Madelyn! Honest I'm not," I said. I was afraid she would roll over and lie on her side again. She didn't. But she didn't say anything either.

"You told Mother 'bout him. Why won't you tell me?"

"Mother doesn't call him 'that drippy boy.' "

"I won't either. Especially if you tell me his name."

Madelyn's long breath was different this time. Kind of musical.

"Marcus. Marcus Harris."

"What?"

"Marcus Harris. That's his name."

I waited for more.

"And, he's…he's really fine. A dream."

I kept on waiting. It was paying off.

"He's a senior, and even though I'm only a sophomore, I know he likes me."

I tried to keep waiting, but there were things I just had to ask. "How do you know that? You only been in school a week. How'd you get to know what he's thinkin' already?"

"I didn't just meet him, Amanda." Madelyn started pulling at her hair and playing with it again. "I saw him around last year at school, and this summer he worked in Dad's office building. I'd see him whenever I went over there, and we'd talk. Sometimes."

Our father is a lawyer. He owns an office building with Alicia and Edna's father, who's a dentist. Me and Alicia and Edna asked our fathers if we could work in their offices this summer like Madelyn did, but they said no. Our dads must think that just because we're in fifth grade, we don't know enough to answer the phone and put stuff in drawers under the right letter of the alphabet. Because that's all Madelyn did while she worked there.

Madelyn kept pulling at her hair while she talked about Marcus. "He's *really* nice, and very cool." She grabbed her Delta pillow and started hugging it.

Both Madelyn and I have Delta pillows on our beds. They're red and shaped like a triangle and have funny white letters on them. When Mother gave us the pillows, she said the colors and the letters represent her sorority. Delta Sigma Theta. That's why we call them Delta pillows. But it looked like Madelyn was ready to call hers a Marcus pillow.

"You'd like him, Amanda," she said in a long, musical-breath voice. "He also has a sister who's about your age. Her name's Ernestine."

I was about to ask her why she thought I would like him just because he has a sister the same age as me. Then it hit me. Ernestine. Ernestine Harris. That was probably the Ernestine who went to Miss Elder's. It had to be.

I wanted to make sure. "Did you say Marcus's sister's name is Ernestine?" I said. "Ernestine Harris?"

"Yeah, that's what he said," Madelyn answered, clutching that dumb pillow. "Do you know her?"

How about that. Fatso Ernestine Harris was Marcus's sister. Marcus who was supposed to be so fine and cool. Right.

Not if he looked anything like his fatso sister.

I was about to bust out laughing when the Voices started. They hadn't started at dinner like they had almost every night lately, so I was beginning to think we were going to be safe. But they were starting now. Were they ever.

"Look, Elizabeth, I don't care what—"

"That's the problem in a nutshell, George. You don't care at all!"

"How can you say that? You haven't been listening to a thing I've been saying. Not one thing!"

"That's all I do, George. Listen to you. Over and over and over."

Madelyn turned over to lie on her side. I felt like crawling next to her to be close, but I didn't. I stayed at the bottom of her bed. I wanted to put my hands over my ears. But I didn't do that either.

The only thing I did do was press my lips together while I

forced the air from my mouth into my ears. If I pushed hard enough, I could shut out the Voices. This worked the best if I said something inside my head while I pushed the air. So I did.

Shut up, Mother. Shut up, Dad. Shut up. Shut up. Shut up. SHUT UP!

5 ✒ *Ernestine*

"UMMM-UM! Louise, you fix the best collard greens in the absolute world!"

Uncle J. B. reached across the dining room table to get his third helping of greens. I had passed the bowl to him two times already, so I knew.

I love it when Uncle J. B. comes over for dinner. Besides being my favorite relative, he likes good food as much as I do. He's a lucky eater too. He can eat as much as he wants of anything without gaining one single pound! I wish I were a lucky eater, but I'm not.

I wanted to ask Jazz to pass the rolls, but if I did she'd say something. She'd already passed them to me twice, and I knew she was keeping count just like I was. I had to figure out a way to get my rolls without passing by her big mouth.

"Quit tryin' to stuff me, J. B.," Mama said. Her smile was real twinkly. Mama loves hearing how good her cooking is.

"I'll give you the same amount of greens to take home no matter what you say. So stop wasting that sweet talk on me."

"Yeah, Uncle J. B.," Jazz said, "quit stuffin' Mama and tell us some more about the...the, ah, what is it?"

"Jabberwock. Is that what you want to know more about, Miss Jazz?"

"What is the Jabberwock?" Jazz asked.

Jazz could care less about the...whatever it was. All she was doing was stalling. She was through with her dinner and knew that after dinner we were supposed to go and do our homework or read or something. But Jazz was going to play it to the end. Till Mama or Daddy told her to get going.

And I wasn't going to be able to get more rolls until she did.

"Why don't you tell your daughters about the Jabberwock, Louise," Daddy said. "It's *your* organization that gives it every year."

"And it's *your* organization that's been winning it every year for the past five years," Mama said back to Daddy. "So I'd think you'd have plenty to say about it yourself."

"I wish *somebody* would tell me *something*," Jazz said. To me, her voice sounded awfully close to yelling. The way Mama looked at Jazz, I think she thought so, too.

Jazz picked up on Mama's look, too. "Tell me about the Jabberwock, Mama. Please?" she said in a soppy voice.

Mama sat back in her chair. Like she was proud.

"The Jabberwock is an event, Jazz," she said. "We have it every year as a way to raise money."

"Who's 'we,' Mama?"

"My sorority." Mama had a big smile on her face. "Delta Sigma Theta."

Marcus reached over Jazz to pick up the plate of rolls. "Do we have any more rolls in the kitchen, Mama?" he asked. "Hot ones?"

"Yep. There're some I'm keeping warm in the oven."

Marcus pushed his chair back, getting ready to get up. My chance had come.

I reached for the plate. "I'll get them, big brother," I said.

The swinging door between the dining room and kitchen didn't shut all the way. But that was okay. I'd still be able to snatch a couple of rolls and hear the conversation.

"...I'm not exactly sure where the name comes from, Jazz," I heard Mama say, "although I know that "Jabber-wocky" is a poem from the *Alice in Wonderland* tale."

"And maybe *you* can tell us about that, Jazz."

I wanted to laugh when I heard Daddy say that. I figured maybe now Jazz would shut up. But I figured wrong.

"What does Jabberwocky mean to your...ah, sorry T?"

Everybody laughed when Jazz said that. I stuffed a roll in my mouth.

"So-ror-i-ty," Mama said real slow. "Delta Sigma Theta is a...it's my sorority, which is an organization made up of women."

"Like a fraternity is an organization made up of men," Daddy said. "Such as Omega Psi Phi, the fraternity both your Uncle J. B. and I belong to."

I knew Jazz didn't care about all that stuff any more than I did. But she would keep on sitting there acting like she did.

I was popping another roll in my mouth when Marcus

called. "Ernestine, where are those rolls?"

"Yeah, Ernestine," Jazz called right after Marcus, "where are the rolls? Are they in your stomach?"

I wanted to run into the dining room and choke her. But before I did I would have to get rid of the roll that was still stuffed in my mouth. I wouldn't be able to chew it fast enough, so I just blew the whole wad toward the trash can. I missed.

"Is there a problem, Ernestine?" Mama called.

"No, ma'am," I said. I pushed through the door with the plate filled with warm rolls I had taken from the oven.

"Sorry it took me so long. I couldn't find the pot holder at first," I said with my fingers crossed under the plate.

Jazz looked at me funny, but I ignored her.

I had to get back in the kitchen to clean up around the trash can. "I'm going to take the rest of the rolls out of the oven so they won't get hard," I said.

"Thanks, baby," Mama said.

While I cleaned up the mess, I could hear Mama and Daddy and Uncle J. B. telling Jazz more about the Jabber-wock stuff. How the Deltas had it every year as a way to raise money for scholarships. How they had been putting it on forever. Since the 1920s. How Mama's Delta group made the Jabberwock a competition between all the other sorori-ties and fraternities in town. And how Daddy's fraternity, the Omegas, had been winning the competition forever. For the past five years.

Jazz was having to sit there listening to all that boring stuff and pretend to be interested. "That's what you get. Goody for you, Jazz," I said to the oven, where I was stand-ing with the last of the rolls.

I was about ready go back into the dining room when it sounded like they were finally talking about something else. I decided to have one last roll before I left the kitchen. This one with lots of butter.

Sometimes, when I do dishes or something and it's getting dark outside, I can see myself in the window above the kitchen sink. That's how I watched myself biting into the roll. And that's where I saw IT.

The butter on the roll started dripping down from the roll. It fell in one big glop on my chin, making it greasy and shiny. Making it look fat.

I moved my face closer to the window mirror. My chin *was* fat. My *face* was fat. *I* was fat.

All of a sudden the roll didn't taste so good. I threw the rest of it in the trash can. Then I looked in the window mirror about the sink again to give myself a message.

Stop eating so much, Ernestine. Stop, stop, STOP!

October

6 ✒ Amanda

A STUPID GRIN had been on Alicia's face ever since we left Miss Elder's. It was really beginning to get on my nerves. Especially seeing it stay there while we plowed through the crunchy dead leaves and hopped over sidewalk cracks to keep from having bad luck.

I just had to say something. "Alicia! Girl, why you keep grinning like that?"

"Alicia's thinkin' about winning that competition," Edna said, starting to laugh. I started, too.

"Whach'all laughin' at?" Alicia said. The grin was leaving her face. Finally.

"You oughta know," I said. "You been grinnin' like a fool ever since we left Miss Elder's. Are you *really* thinking about winnin' that stupid competition?"

Alicia stopped walking and started yelling. *Yelling.* Alicia never yelled. I could hardly believe it.

"What if I was, Amanda?" she said. "What would be wrong with that? And what's so 'stupid' about the competition anyhow?"

"How come you standin' there yellin'?" I said, looking at her.

Edna was the one who had started talking about winning that dumb competition. Now Alicia, my always-best-friend, was standing there, yelling at *me!* I just couldn't believe it!

"Well, Amanda?" Alicia said. Her face was right in front of mine.

"Well, what?" I said.

"Why don't you tell me what's so stupid about Miss Elder's competition?"

I really didn't think the competition was all that stupid, but it was stupid to be thinking about it. In the first place, it wasn't for sure yet that Miss Elder was going to have it, and if she did, it wouldn't be until May, and that would be almost time for school to let out. And school had only just started. Only about a month ago!

But it was *super* stupid to be thinking about winning it. Of course Alicia would win. Nobody else who took piano lessons from Miss Elder played as good as Alicia. Not even Edna. Anyhow, Alicia would practice her head off like she always did, and Edna wouldn't. Every time Edna sat down to practice, she ended up playing boogie-woogie. If Miss Elder was having a boogie-woogie contest, Edna would win without practicing one lick. But Alicia would win any other kind of piano-playing competition.

So what was the big deal about winning?

"I'm still waiting, Amanda."

Alicia was still in my face. "Alicia, what is wrong with you?" I said. "You actin' like you got a problem. I only said—"

"I know what you said," Alicia said, cutting me off. "You said 'stupid' competition. That's what you said."

Now I was getting mad.

"And it is! Not the competition so much, but worrying about winning *is* stupid."

"You're the one sayin' I'm worrying about winning," Alicia said. She hadn't lowered her voice one bit. "All I'm doing is thinking about being in the competition, *which*, by the way, I think is a great idea."

"Nobody said it wasn't," I said. "And any of Miss Elder's students with half a brain oughta know that you will *win* it."

Alicia wasn't exactly yellin' anymore, but she was still in my face. "Like I said, Amanda, winning isn't what I'm thinkin' about," she said. "But even if it was, who's to say it'll be me. There's Brenda Wilson, and there's Ernestine and—"

"Ernestine?" I cut Alicia off fast. "Ernestine Harris? Fatso Ernestine Harris? Alicia, she can't even read music."

"What are you talking about 'she can't read music'?" Alicia started yelling again. "Haven't you heard Ernestine play? 'Cause if you have, you must know she's fantastic!"

I couldn't believe what I was hearing. I wanted to tell Alicia that she didn't know what *she* was talking about, but she wouldn't shut up.

"And what *is* your problem, Amanda? Why are you sayin' mean things about Ernestine?" Alicia was really yellin' now. "You don't even know her. And anyhow, she's not all that fat!"

"She is *so* all that fat," I said. Now I was yelling, too. "And I know when someone is good on the piano, too, and that somebody is *not* Fatso Ernestine Harris."

I had said all I really wanted to say, but I was not going to let Alicia have the last word!

"And *you're* the one with a problem, Alicia," I yelled. "A problem as fat as Ernestine!"

I started running down the street. I didn't care how many sidewalk cracks I stepped on, and I didn't stop until I got home.

I was still mad when I sat down for dinner. And I still couldn't believe how mad Alicia had gotten at *me*. I hadn't done anything.

Not only that, Alicia was taking up for Ernestine. Ernestine Fatso Harris. I couldn't believe any of this.

I decided that after dinner I would go over to Alicia and Edna's house. Since they only live next door, I could go over for a little while and still have time to do my homework.

I knew exactly what I was going to do when I got there. I would ignore Alicia. I would only talk to Edna. I'd only tell Edna what Rodney had said to me today. Then Alicia would know how it felt to have your best friend do something that made you feel bad.

Just wait, Alicia. You'll see.

I hurried up to clean my plate even though mostly meat loaf and peas were left on it, two foods I hate. Just when I was almost ready to ask to be excused from the table, Dad started talking. I couldn't believe it. Up to then he hadn't said one word. No one had except Madelyn who complained about having to eat meat loaf.

"How was your music lesson?" Dad said. I knew he was talking to me but he was looking at Mother.

"It was okay," I said. I was going to tell them about Miss Elder's competition, but it would take too long. I'd tell them later. I wanted to leave.

"How did your chemistry test turn out?" Dad said. I knew he was talking to Madelyn this time, but he was still looking at Mother.

"We won't get our papers back until tomorrow," Madelyn said. She wasn't looking at anything but the glob of meat loaf on her plate.

I finished eating. Finally. "Can I be excused?" I asked. I had already started pushing back my chair.

"What's your hurry?" Dad said. This time he was looking at me. "I thought we might talk for a while."

"About what?"

"Anything you want," Dad said. "What would you like to talk about?"

I didn't want to talk about anything. I wanted to go next door.

"I think your father wants us to spend some family time together," Mother said. It didn't sound like she was talking to Dad, but she was looking at him.

Then Mother pushed her chair away from the table. "So, please, girls, talk with your father. Talk with him about... about *family* things."

Mother went into the kitchen.

Dad got up from the table. "Elizabeth?" he called to my mother.

My stomach began to feel like the meat loaf and peas had landed there in one big lump. *They* were getting ready to start.

I looked at Madelyn. She was still pushing the meat loaf around on her plate. Then she rushed away from the table like she did when she had heard the phone ringing. But the phone wasn't ringing. Nothing was ringing. Everything was quiet. But I knew things would be getting loud soon. Very soon.

All of a sudden I noticed that I was the only one left at the table. I was the one who had wanted to leave in the first place, and now everybody had gone but me. And now I didn't care if I left or not.

7 ❧ Ernestine

MY LESSON WITH Miss Elder had been very long. We had gone over practically everything twice. Even when we finished I knew I wasn't through for the day. Miss Elder had asked everybody to wait until all the lessons were over so she could talk to us.

When I came out of the lesson room, the waiting hall was practically full. I noticed an almost empty chair next to Alicia, and she took her book and coat off the chair when she saw me. "Thanks, Alicia, " I said, and sat down.

Alicia is really nice. She isn't anything like I used to think she was. Stuck up like her friend Amanda.

Amanda was sitting at one end of the row of chairs. She and Edna had been whispering ever since I came in.

I started looking in my lesson book. I didn't want Alicia to feel like she had to talk to me just because I was sitting next to her. But I could tell that she was looking at me, so I had to say something.

"Your sister better watch out. Old Dragon Breath's liable to come in here and breathe all over her," I said.

"Who?" Alicia said.

I had forgotten that only Clovis and I knew who Dragon Breath was.

"Dragon Breath. Mrs. Elder." I said. "Her breath'll kill you just like a dragon would, don't you think?"

Alicia's eyes got real wide. Then she burst out laughing.

I put my hand over my mouth to try hold back my laugh. "Shhhh," I said through my fingers.

Alicia put her hand over her mouth, too. "Dragon Breath!" she whispered from behind her hand. "That's even better than 'the Warden.'"

"Is that what you call her?" I said, whispering, too.

"Yeah. That's what we all call her—me and Amanda and Edna. You know, 'cause she's always actin' like a guard or something. Watching every move we make while we're sittin' in here."

"I think she's nosy, too," I said, leaning closer to Alicia. "She's always asking questions about stuff."

"She's nosy, all right," Alicia said. She leaned so close to me I could smell her skin. It smelled like lemons. "She asks a lot of questions and then gets on the phone and gossips about everything she hears."

"How do you know that?"

"'Cause she gossips a lot to my grandmother," Alicia said, "and sometimes I hear Grandmother gossiping to Mommy about some of the stuff."

We both started laughing again. And hitting each other with our elbows to try to keep from laughing.

I looked over at the door leading to the sunporch. I expected to see old Dragon Breath standing there, staring and ready to stomp in to yell at me and Alicia for talking and laughing. But she wasn't.

Who I *did* see staring was Amanda. She had this real mean look on her face. Like she was mad at me and Alicia or something. Then I figured she was probably mad because Alicia and I were laughing and talking together. That *her* good friend was having fun with me.

I felt like sticking out my tongue at her.

So much for you, Miss Stuck-up.

All of us sitting there in the hall had finished our lessons and were waiting. Me, Alicia, Edna, and Amanda. Lynn Thompson and Marvin Cobb were there, too. They had been waiting longer than anybody. Brenda Wilson was having her lesson, and she was the last one.

When Brenda came out of the teaching room, Miss Elder came out behind her.

"Thank you for being so patient," Miss Elder said. She pulled up one of the empty chairs and sat down in front of us. Brenda sat down on the other side of me.

"I've heard from Camille Nickerson, and it's all set. She will definitely be coming in the spring to give a recital."

Miss Elder had this big grin on her face, and her eyes were sparkly shiny. "And," she said, "Miss Nickerson has agreed to feature one of my students in the concert."

Miss Elder's smile was like a big sun making you feel nice and warm. I felt like she was talking just to me. I could tell by the look on Alicia's face that she felt the same way.

Brenda Wilson raised her hand, just like we were in school or something. "Is that why you're having the contest you were talking about, Miss Elder? To see who'll play with Miss Nickerson?" she asked.

"I regret that we have to think of it as a 'contest,'" Miss Elder said with a little laugh. It was like a tweet of a little bird. "But I suppose that's what it is. A competition or contest of sorts."

Miss Elder moved around in her chair like she wasn't comfortable. "But then, I suppose that's only fair since Camille—ah, Miss Nickerson is a much-respected musician," she said.

"Is she famous all over the world?" asked Lynn Thompson.

"Miss Nickerson is well known in the music community." Miss Elder sounded like a teacher explaining something in school. "She comes from a family of musicians, has studied at Juilliard, one of the finest schools in America, and has traveled widely, both in America and abroad."

I had never even heard of Camille Nickerson before, but just thinking about playing on the same stage as somebody famous was making me nervous. Then I felt my insides kinda laughing. What was I worried about! I couldn't win Miss Elder's competition even if I wanted to. And I didn't think I wanted to.

"When will the contest be, Miss Elder?" Alicia's voice was whispery.

"We haven't picked an exact date yet, but it will be soon after Miss Nickerson comes to town." Miss Elder looked like she was enjoying talking to us again.

"Where will the contest be?" Amanda asked in her stuck-up voice. "The same place as the recital?"

"Miss Nickerson's recital will be in the high school auditorium. Benjamin Banneker High," Miss Elder said. "But the, ah, competition will probably be here, in my studio."

"Hey, Miss Elder, who's gonna be the judge?" Marvin says "Hey" to everybody, but it sounded funny to hear him say that to Miss Elder. She didn't seem to mind though.

"Miss Nickerson for certain, Marvin," she said, and winked at him, "and maybe me, too. I haven't worked out all the details yet and want all of you and my other students to work with me to make the plans."

Miss Elder stood up. "In the meantime, we can all think about the very special day we'll have this spring," she said. "And all of us will take part in the event, no matter who's chosen to play with Miss Nickerson."

"Miss Elder, I think we should all wear long dresses, " Edna said. She started patting and fussing with her hair. This is something she does a lot.

"That's a wonderful idea, Edna!" Miss Elder said, looking at Edna with one of her sun smiles. "It will make the event extra special."

Long gowns? Playing in the high school auditorium? Now I know I don't want to be in that recital.

"And then Edna said she thought everybody should wear long dresses," I said.

Clovis had called right after dinner. He said he was calling about history homework, but I knew he was calling to find out what had gone on at Miss Elder's like he did practically every Wednesday after my piano lesson.

Clovis wants to know everything about everybody. It isn't that he likes to gossip or anything, although he and I talk about practically everything. But he does like finding out about people a lot more than I do. And ever since I started telling him about Alicia and Edna and Miss Stuck-up Know-Everything-in-the-World Amanda, he asked me about them all the time.

None of them went to the same school Clovis and I go to, so he didn't really know them. Except for music lessons, I didn't know them either. But Alicia and Edna's father was Clovis's dentist, so he knew who they were the first time I mentioned them. I figured that's why he wanted to know stuff about them. I couldn't figure out any reason somebody would want to know about Amanda.

"What did Miss Elder say? Will everybody have to dress up?" Clovis wanted every detail.

"I don't know," I said. "All I know is that I won't be dressin' up in no—ugh—long gown."

"How come?"

" 'Cause I just won't." I was getting tired of this conversation.

" 'Cause you think you can't win the contest?" Clovis asked. Then his voice got even more serious than usual. "Because you can, Ernestine. You play the piano better than anybody I know, and I bet anything you play a whole lot better than any of them."

"You just think so 'cause you're my friend," I said. "But even if I could, I can't imagine myself even sitting on the stage in the high school auditorium. That's a whole lot different than a church stage."

Clovis didn't say anything, and I was about ready to

change the subject. Then he said something else.

"It's a long time before spring, Ernestine. You can do a lot before then. Even lose weight if you want to."

Sometimes it's a real pain to have a friend who thinks he can read your mind.

8 ❧ Amanda

IT WAS A LOT colder outside than it looked. Too cold to not even be Halloween yet, and definitely too cold to be standing outside with only my green sweater on, even though it's the warmest sweater I have. I was freezing, so I rang the doorbell again. Edna opened the door. Finally.

"What took you so long? It's gettin' cold outside." I started blowing my breath on my fingers.

"Sorry. Mommy just said, 'See who's at the door.' I thought Alicia was going, and she thought I was."

Sometimes it really gets on my nerves hearing Edna and Alicia calling their mother "Mommy," like they're little kids or something. I've wanted to say something to Alicia about it, but never have. Sometimes I think I should. It would be better for her to hear something like that from her best friend.

"Where's Alicia?" I asked. I looked around. The only

thing I saw moving was a fire in the fireplace in the living room.

"I dunno. I been doing my social studies homework," Edna said, going into the living room. She held up her hand in that come-follow-me way.

The Raymonds have a pretty house. I think it's almost as pretty as ours, but Madelyn thinks ours is much prettier. She said that Mother told her our house had been built first and that Mrs. Raymond had copied a lot of things when they built theirs. Madelyn said that no copy can be as good as the original.

Our two houses *are* a lot alike. They both have a little hall you step into as soon as you walk through the front door. You have to take one step up to get to the living room. Both houses have the dining room on the other side of the living room and a swinging door that leads to the kitchen. And both of them have a long hall that leads from the living room to the other rooms on the first floor and to the stairway going up to the second floor.

But after that, the houses aren't alike at all. We have carpeting everywhere. Even on the steps going upstairs. You can see most of the wood on the Raymonds' floors, although some rooms have rugs. Mrs. Raymond calls them 'oriental rugs,' whatever that means. And there's different statues and masks all over the place. Dr. Raymond calls them his African treasures. Madelyn and I call them weird.

One good thing about the Raymonds' house is that Mrs. Raymond doesn't carry on about stuff like Mother does. Stuff like, "Make sure you stay in the kitchen while you're eating that sandwich," or, "Why don't you read in your room so we can keep the living room straight." And there would never be a real fire in our fireplace. Mother says the ashes and smoke mess up the carpeting. We have fake logs that nobody ever lights.

Mother would probably have had a fit if I did what Edna did when we went into the living room. She stretched out on the couch with her shoes still on and started eating potato chips.

"Wansom 'ips?" she said.

Sometimes Edna really gets on my nerves. Like then. Talking with her mouth so full I could hardly make out what she was saying.

"Have you forgotten that we're supposed to be planning the party? Are you ready to get started?" I said.

I had come over to talk about the Halloween party we were going to have. We all decided we'd get together tonight, after everyone finished dinner. But it was beginning to look like I was the only one who remembered.

"A-LEE-sha!" Edna yelled so loud that little bits of potato chips flew out of her mouth.

"Watch out, girl!" I said, rubbing my hand on the arm of the chair. It felt like some of Edna's spitty chips had hit it.

" 'Scuse me, Amanda," Edna said. She stuffed more chips in her mouth.

Alicia came downstairs. Finally. "Hi, Amanda," she said.

"Did you forget we were going to get together?" I said. Alicia had been so picky lately, I tried not to sound angry.

"I didn't forget. Did you forget, Edna?" Alicia pushed her sister's legs off the couch to make a place to sit down.

"How come you think I forgot? I been sittin' down here

waiting," Edna said, pushing back at Alicia with her feet.

"You were *not* waiting. You been sittin' in here doin' your homework 'cause Mommy said you'd be in trouble if you didn't." Alicia started tickling Edna's feet.

"Stop it!" Edna said, jerking her feet back.

You could tell that Edna and Alicia weren't really mad at each other, even though they were acting like it. For one thing, their voices weren't mad sounding. And I knew exactly what Alicia's mad-sounding voice was like because lately I had been hearing it a lot.

"So, let's talk about the party," Alicia said. "Where should we have it?"

We all looked at each other. I didn't want to be the first to say anything, but I thought I'd better.

"I think we should have it here," I said. "At your house."

Alicia and Edna looked at me like they were waiting for me to say something else. So I did.

"Your basement is better for a party than ours," I said.

I felt like I had to keep on explaining. "I know our basements are a lot alike, but Mother is having some work done in ours, and it might not be finished in time for the party."

And the way Mother and Dad are carrying on lately I don't want a lot of people coming to our house.

"No big deal," Edna said. "I don't think Mommy or Daddy will mind."

"Since we're going to have it here, we could ask Daddy to make some of his spicy chili," Edna said. "We can ask him to make it real spicy and then call it 'Devil's Stew.'"

"I can't eat real spicy food, Edna," I said. "Have you forgotten?"

"That's not the only thing we'll have," Alicia said. "We can have hot dogs, too."

"And potato chips, and popcorn, and pop, and—"

"And apples that we can bob for!"

"Great idea, Amanda." Alicia got up from the couch and went over to the desk. "I'm gonna start writing this down so we won't forget."

"I'll ask Mother to make a cake," I said. My mother makes scrumptious cakes. "And she can decorate it with Halloween stuff."

Alicia was sitting at the desk and had started making the list. I sat in the chair next to the desk. Edna was still piling potato chips in her mouth, and I didn't want to get hit again.

Alicia is very organized. Her side of their bedroom is always neat, with everything put away in a special place. Edna says that when they clean up their room, like they have to do every Saturday, Alicia walks around humming a silly song she made up when they were little:

> Everything has its face,
> Everything has its place.
> Nothing should leave a trace,
> Erase the mess, erase.

I've never heard the song, but I can imagine Alicia making it up and singing it. Sometimes she's so neat it gets on my nerves.

Like making the list. First she had printed **FOOD** in big letters. Under it she wrote all of the foods we had named. She even left space to add more things later before she wrote the word **GAMES** in big letters. Under that she wrote **bob for apples** and then left lots more space. She had started drawing pictures of heads next to the word **PEOPLE.**

"OK," she said, "now we get to the best part. The guest list."

"Anybody but Cissy Greene," Edna said. "I can't stand her."

"And Nesta Rogers," I said. "Nobody can stand her."

"Nobody can stand any of those Rogers kids," Edna said. She had finished the bag of potato chips. Finally.

Alicia was writing something under **PEOPLE.** "Whose names you puttin' down?" I asked her. "I think we should all agree about who we invite."

Alicia kept writing. "I'm writing down Bobby Wilson and his sister Pearl," she said. "Even you and Edna like them."

Alicia sounded like she was getting touchy again. But her face looked regular. I decided not to say anything.

Edna came over to look at the list. "Bobby and Pearl are fun," she said. "So is Pamela Tolliver and Jessie Knox. Put their names down."

"You know who else is fun?" Alicia said. She was adding curls to one of the heads she had drawn. "Ernestine."

"Ernestine? Ernestine from Miss Elder's?" I could hardly believe what I was hearing.

"Yes, Ernestine." Alicia stopped drawing. "And her name is Ernestine Harris, not Ernestine From-Miss-Elder's."

I had sure been right. Alicia *was* getting touchy. And she was getting on my nerves in a BIG way.

"Well," I said, "I don't agree that we should invite Ernestine *whatever*-her-name-is. In the first place we hardly know her, and in the second place, she wouldn't know hardly anybody else here. She doesn't go to our school. The only time we ever see her is at piano lessons."

"And in the third place, she'd probably eat all the food up," Edna said, laughing.

I laughed too, but Alicia didn't. She didn't even smile. In fact, she started getting mad.

"Sometimes you two make me sick," she said. She slammed her pencil down on the desk. "You don't even know Ernestine, so how can you talk so mean about her?"

Alicia got up from the chair. "Invite whoever you want. I don't care," she said. Then she left the room.

I could hardly believe it. "What on earth is wrong with her?" I said. The pencil she had thrown down was rolling across the desk. I stopped it before it rolled off. Then I sat down in the chair Alicia had zoomed out of like a crazy person.

"Got me," Edna said. She flopped down in the chair I had gotten out of. "Mommy says sometimes Alicia tries to have an artist's temperament, whatever that means."

"It means she's getting on *everyone's* nerves," I said. Edna and I both laughed.

"Go ahead, let's finish the list," Edna said. "You heard Alicia. She doesn't care who we invite."

"Well, I do, and that means Miss Fatso Ernestine Hairless *won't* be on the list." I erased the **E** of the name Alicia had started writing.

"I don't know how come Alicia wants to invite Ernestine," I said. I made sure all the eraser flakes were brushed off the paper. "She doesn't even live near us. Where does she live anyhow?"

"I dunno," Edna said. "But probably over near Jackson

Street. You know, on the other side of Miss Elder's. She must live that close to Miss Elder's 'cause she walks to her lesson usually."

"Then she probably goes to Fourth Street Elementary. That's a dumpy school."

Edna threw her legs across the arm of the chair. "You said that we should all agree about who to invite, and I agree. No Ernestine. No *anybody* who goes to dumpy Fourth Street Elementary," she said.

I looked at the paper to make sure that there was no trace of the **E** name. "This is going to be the best guest list ever. And the best *party* ever," I said. "Just wait. You'll see."

And you will too, Miss Temperamental Alicia. Just wait. You'll see.

November

9 ✒ *Ernestine*

"ERNESTINE, WHY DON'T you wait on that second piece of pie, baby. It'll make a good snack, if you still want it later."

Mama was whispering in my ear. I hadn't even realized she was in the room. But there were so many people packed in the house for Thanksgiving dinner, it was hard to know who was anywhere.

"Good idea, Mama. That's what I'll do."

I pulled my hand away from the sweet potato pie. There were only two pieces left on the plate, but I figured I'd be able to grab one of them and wrap it up to take to my room as soon as Mama went out of the room again. There was almost a whole apple pie left on the other plate, but it was a pie that Aunt Millie had made. And her pies are terrible.

It had been our turn to have the family Thanksgiving dinner, so the house was packed with as much food as people. People and food were in practically every room. I had even seen my little cousins Corey and Carol eating their dessert in the bathroom!

I love Thanksgiving. It's a real five-sense day: I can see it, hear it, feel it, smell it, and taste it. I get to see all my relatives and hear them laughing, talking. There are lots of hugs (and some wet kisses, unfortunately—ugh). All kinds of make-your-stomach-rumble smells spread all over the house, even early in the morning. And I can taste Thanksgiving dinner forever!

This year there seemed to be more Harrises (relatives on my father's side) and Morgans (relatives on my mother's side) than ever. I figure that's because my mama's the best cook of any Harris or Morgan. I know Uncle J. B. would agree with me, and he's a Harris!

I had seen Uncle J. B. eyeing those last two pieces of sweet potato pie, too, so I figured I'd better say something to him. Fast.

"Uncle J. B., Mama's pie sure is good, huh."

"As good as a waterfall in the desert is to a thirsty man!" Uncle J. B. leaned over and whispered in my ear. "And so much better than Aunt Millie's, it's a cryin' shame."

Uncle J. B. and I laughed.

Even though Uncle J. B. is my father's brother, Daddy says Uncle J. B. is also his best friend. Mama says that the two of them live each other's lives. I don't know what she means, but she says it all the time.

"I saw you eyeballing those last two pieces of the pie, Ernestine," Uncle J. B. said, "so I'm here to make a deal with you."

"What kind of deal?"

"A delicious kind of a deal." Uncle J. B. gave me one of his "sweet lady" smiles. That's what Jazz and I call those smiles he always puts on whenever he's with one of his lady friends.

"I'll take this pie plate into the kitchen and wrap up each piece," he said, "one for you, and one for me."

"And for my part of the deal, I won't tell anyone." I couldn't keep from laughing.

"Listen to you," Uncle J. B. said, laughing, too. "Tryin' to be slick." He reached across the table and picked up the pie plate. "For your part of the deal, you'll play a little something for us on the piano," he said.

"No deal, no deal!" I said. In my head I said good-bye to that last piece of pie.

I tried to wiggle out from under Uncle J. B.'s arm, but he wouldn't let me. "Come on, Ernestine," he said. "Everybody looks forward to hearing you play."

"Uncle J. B., it's not fair. Every time we all get together, someone asks me to get up in front of everybody and, you know, perform." I looked right up into Uncle J. B.'s face. "You know, like I'm a little kid or something."

Uncle J. B. pulled me over next to the wall where nobody was standing. He bent down so he could look right into my face.

"Ernestine," he said, "you *are* a kid. Not a little kid, and not just any kid. You're my niece who has been blessed with a wonderful talent. A God-given talent put there to be shared. And who better to share it with than your family— the people who love you most?"

Uncle J. B.'s sweet-lady smile was all over his face. It was even in his shiny eyes that were saying, "I'm tellin' you the truth, Ernestine."

"So, whadda you say, sweet-potato buddy—do we have a deal?"

"We have a deal." I reached up to kiss Uncle J. B. on his cheek.

"That's my girl!"

Uncle J. B. went in the kitchen to wrap up the pie. I went to the bathroom to wipe off my sweaty hands. When I came out, I heard my brother, Marcus, on the telephone.

He was talking louder than he usually talks on the phone, probably because of all the talking already in the house. So I didn't have any trouble hearing what he was saying. I didn't even have to hide and practically hold my breath to hear him like I have to do sometimes when he's carrying on with one of his girlfriends.

"I should be able to cut out from here in about thirty minutes. What about you?"

Marcus was brushing his hair with his hand. He was doing it good, too. As much time as he spends in front of the bathroom mirror, he probably had every picture of himself memorized.

"Won't Amanda help you out? She's your sister—isn't that what sisters do for each other?"

Amanda? Marcus was going with a girl who had a sister named Amanda?

"Aw, c'mon, Madelyn. I really want to see you tonight. It's a holiday—"

Madelyn? Alicia said that Miss Stuck-up had a sister named Madelyn. Could it be…?

"Great! I'll be over to pick you up in about forty-five minutes." Marcus dropped his voice. "See you soon, baby." He hung up the phone.

"Marcus!" My voice came out so loud it almost made *me* jump. It *did* make Marcus jump. He almost stumbled going up the steps.

"Marcus, is your girlfriend's name Madelyn Clay?" I asked him.

"Not that it's any of your business, but yeah." Then Marcus actually smiled. Any other time he would have growled at me for trying to get in his business. He must have really been in love.

"And her sister's name is Amanda Clay?"

The silly smile stayed on Marcus's face. "You were listening to me on the phone, so you already know," he said.

"What I know is that you messin' with a girl who's got a stuck-up sister. That's what I know!"

"How do you know Amanda?" Marcus said. He wasn't bothered one bit by the facts I was giving him. "Oh, yeah. You and Amanda are probably in the same grade at school."

"For your kind information, that stuck-up, *un*-nice girl does not even go to my school."

"Then, how do you figure you know so much about her?" Marcus said, leaning over the banister.

"Because she takes music lessons the same time I do at Miss Elder's." I moved closer to Marcus. "Do you really like her sister, Marcus?" I asked.

"I really do," he said. He reached over to touch my nose. "And so will you. I'm gonna bring her over here in a little while."

"You *are?*"

"I am, and you'll have a chance to see for yourself what I'm talking about." Marcus went on up the steps, taking two at a time.

This was turning into a Thanksgiving nightmare. I had promised Uncle J. B. that I would play something on the piano. And now, stuck-up Amanda would probably walk in while I was playing. Walk in and snicker at me like she did every time we were in the same room. And if she snickered at me in my own house I would punch her stuck-up face right off her evil neck!

I yelled up the stairs. "Marcus, is Madelyn the only one you're bringing over here?"

"I'll ask Amanda to come too, if you want me to," he yelled back.

"Nooooooo, no!" I started up the stairs.

"Ernestine, is something wrong?" Aunt Kitty caught my arm.

"Nothing, Aunt Kitty," I said. I stopped on the second step.

"Good, because J. B. just told us we were in for a treat. That you're going to play for us."

Aunt Kitty is really sweet. Next to Uncle J. B. she's my favorite not-in-the-house relative. If anybody else had been standing there I might have said I had changed my mind. But I couldn't say that to Aunt Kitty.

"And I wanna play now." I figured I might as well get it over with. Just in case Marcus lost his mind and really did bring Miss Stuck-up back with him, I could go somewhere in the house where she wasn't and ignore her.

"All right, everyone," Aunt Kitty said, "quiet down. Ernestine's getting ready to play the piano for us." She held up the glass she was holding and started clinking on it with her ring.

Aunt Kitty has a little voice, but she wears gigantic jewelry. Her clinking was like a bell ringing. It made everything quiet down fast. Uncle Court started waving at me with his big fat cigar. "C'mon sugah," he said. "I been lookin' forward to hearin' you play the piano ever since I walked in the door."

I smiled at Uncle Court even though he said practically that same exact thing every time he came to our house.

"You say that all the time, Uncle Court," said Jazz. Miss Big Mouth of twenty countries.

"And I mean it all the time," Uncle Court said back. "Now more than ever, since Ernestine's been taking big-time piano lessons."

Miss Helen was right next to the piano. Seeing her there made me feel funny. Especially after hearing Uncle Court talk about me taking big-time music lessons from Miss Elder.

I could feel a queer smile creeping across my face. A Jazz smile! (I had to do *something* so Miss Helen wouldn't feel bad!) When she put her arm around my shoulder, I got my words ready to pop out. I would tell her that if I messed up it was because I hadn't played with her for a long time.

Then Miss Helen leaned over and whispered in my ear. "I'm so proud of you, Ernestine," she said. "I've been looking forward to hearing you play ever since your mother invited me to join the family for Thanksgiving dinner."

I looked right into Miss Helen's face. Her eyes were shiny

like always. And her smile had as much sun in it as Miss Elder's did. I began to figure that maybe that's how your smile got when you played the piano the best you could.

So that's what I did. I played the best I could.

Everybody clapped when I finished. Some people even cheered. Especially Jazz.

Maybe I will try out in that competition. Alicia said I should. Maybe she's right.

I could see Uncle J. B. smiling at me from across the room. He was eating his piece of pie. He pointed his fork at the pie and then at me. I knew that was his way of telling me that he had saved the other piece of pie for me just like he promised. I smiled back at him.

Mama says that you can keep pie in the freezer for months. That's where I'll keep my piece until after the contest. Till after I'm skinny.

December

10   *Amanda*

December 27, 1955

Dear Edna,

Remember when you said that you would faint if I wrote to you? Well, here's my letter, so faint! (ha-ha)

I can't believe you've been running around every day in a bathing suit. It's so cold and snowy here I can't even go outside. There's so much snow that nobody has gone out but Dad. We've been stuck in the house for almost three whole days! Can you believe it? Madelyn hangs around the phone all the time waiting for that slimy Marcus Harris to call. I keep telling her that he can't call her too much because he has to guard the refrigerator in his house. If he doesn't, his fatso sister will eat up all the food and cause their family to starve to death. (ha-ha)

You're so lucky to have a grandmother who lives in the

Bahamas. I wish mine did. I wish Grandma Nelson lived anywhere else but here. Then I could go away on Christmas to visit someone like you do.

It's been a terrible Christmas. TERRIBLE! Everybody has been in a terrible mood, even Dad. And you know how cheerful he always is. Edna, please, please, pllll-lleeeeeeease don't tell anyone this (especially not your temperamental sister), but sometimes my parents act like they can't stand each other. I think Dad has gone out every day in all this freezing weather just to get away from Mother. He doesn't have to go to his office because he closed it for Christmas week. Whenever he stays in the house, he and Mother fuss at each other or act like the other person isn't even around. It's really terrible. Remember, Edna, please. You promised to keep any secret I tell you, and this is the biggest secret I've ever told anyone. Spit in your hand right now and promise you won't tell. Ever, ever, EVER!

Did you get the locket you wanted for Christmas? I bet you did. Even if you didn't I bet you got something good. Your mom always gives you great presents. Mother has been in such a terrible mood that I didn't expect to get anything good for Christmas, but she actually came through with one great gift. She handed me this huge box wrapped really pretty. When I opened it, all I saw was piles of tissue paper and almost nothing else except this red card. The writing on the card said, "IOU one shopping trip downtown + lunch. Cash this in on a sunny Saturday." I couldn't believe it.

I'm not going to cash it in until you get back so we can

shop together. I know you're planning to get a special dress just like I am for something that's coming up. Something we'll need beautiful new LONG dresses for. Do you know what that could be? (ha-ha)

Madelyn is really getting on my nerves. Ever since I started writing this letter she's been asking me to hurry up and play Speed with her. If I was asking her to play while SHE was writing a letter, she would probably tell me to get lost. Oh well, I guess I'll go since I've written a lot already, and I always beat her.

I'll be glad when you get back, but have a good time anyway. Tell your mom and dad "hi" for me. Bye.

Your friend,
Amanda

P.S. Don't tell your temperamental sister Alicia ANYTHING for me. Especially not "hi."

P.P.S. Tell your grandmother I'd like to visit her sometimes, too. (ha-ha)

January

11 🐦 *Ernestine*

January 1, 1956

Dear Clovis,

Happy New Year!!!!!! Now it REALLY seems like you've been gone forever. Does it seem like that to you, too?

Have you been having a good time in Georgia? I bet it's terrific seeing your father, especially since you haven't seen him for almost a whole year. What's the weather like there? Do you have snow? If you don't, you're lucky. It's been snowing here forever. There's so much snow on the ground it's not even fun to go outside to make a snow castle. Remember the one we made last year? I don't mind not being able to go outside so much, but I do mind Jazz not being able to go out. She is such a PAIN!!!!! While I'm writing to you she's reading over my shoulder and asking me why I'm asking you so many questions in a letter. So I'm going to get up now and lock her out of the room. I'll finish when I get back.

Still January 1

Last night Uncle J. B. had a party at his house to celebrate New Year's. Everybody stayed practically till morning. Even Jazz stayed awake. This morning I slept until almost noon, but not Jazz. She woke up early and walked all over the house singing the song everybody was singing last night at the party. Something about "old Lang's sign." Like I said, Jazz is a GIANT pain!

The party was fun, but I still wonder what's so special about seeing one year end and another one begin. Sheila said I'd understand when I get older. I think that's a dumb thing to say to kids, but I know that she was just trying to be nice. Sheila is Uncle J. B.'s new girlfriend, and she told us to call her Sheila instead of Miss Wilson, which is what Uncle J. B. told us to call her. I think she wants us to like her. I think she thinks that if we like her, Uncle J. B. will, too.

One thing that was really fun was the skits people did. Daddy and Uncle J. B. started everything by talking about what they were going to perform at the Jabberwock. Did I tell you about that? If I didn't, I will when you get back. Anyhow, the rule was that every skit had to be about somebody or something in history. Daddy and Uncle J. B.'s skit was a conversation they pretended took place between somebody called W. E. B. Du Bois and Booker T. Washington. I couldn't understand some of the things they were talking about, but their acting was terrific. Everybody said so.

Still January 1

Sorry to stop and start again, but I had to get a snack. Mama said it's better not to get too hungry because then I'll stuff myself and that I should eat a little bit of something every now and then. So while I'm writing to you I'm munching on some peanuts and leftover Christmas cookies. But only four cookies.

Oops. Sorry about that greasy spot. I'm getting crumbs all over my letter, so I think I'll end. I'll be so glad when you get home.

Wait. There's one more thing. I got a postcard from Alicia! She's visiting her grandmother who lives some place not too far from Florida. Her whole family is there. It was nice of her to send me a card from someplace so far away. Even Jazz was impressed.

See you soon, I hope. Don't be a dope! (I'm a poet and I know it. My feet show it. They're Longfellow. Get it?)

Love,
Ernestine, YBF
(Your Best Friend)

February

12 ✎ *Amanda*

MY FAVORITE ROOM in our house is the piano room. Anyhow, that's what I call it. Mother and Madelyn call it a den because they like to curl up on the couch in there and blab on the telephone. Dad calls it the library because that's where he keeps all his lawyer books. I call it the piano room because that's where our piano is. And the reason I love it is because whenever I'm in there playing the piano, I know I'll be left alone. No one will bother me, not even Madelyn.

Lately I had been spending a lot of time in the piano room. And not just messing around like I did sometimes. Like looking out the window behind the piano and not working hard on my music.

But lately I had been really practicing a lot. I had been working on the piece I was going to play for the competition. It was hard, but it was a perfect piece for winning Miss Elder's contest. Perfect!

I hadn't told anybody what I was going to play. Not even Edna. Not even Miss Elder! The only person who knew was Dad. And that was because he had helped me find the piece in the first place.

One thing about my dad: he's really smart. He knows something about almost everything. He even knew about Camille Nickerson. And nobody I knew besides Miss Elder had even heard of her.

That's what I explained to my dad when I told him about the contest. I said, "I don't think Miss Nickerson's very famous. There's nothing about her in the encyclopedia."

Dad laughed when I said that. "What makes you think that being in the encyclopedia makes you famous?" he asked.

Sometimes Dad asks me questions to see how much I know. I thought this was probably one of those times.

"Well," I said, "the encyclopedia is a reference book. And when you want to find out about something or somebody, you look in a reference book."

"Well," Dad said, "did you ever think about the people who decide who should be listed in the encyclopedia, and who shouldn't?"

I hadn't, but I didn't say anything.

"And that many people who are quite worthy of being listed in a reference source aren't because the people who put together the particular book have chosen not to include them."

"Is that why Miss Nickerson isn't listed in the encyclopedia?" I asked

"Not necessarily," Dad said.

I was really getting confused. I must have had one of

those puzzled looks Dad says I get on my face, because he kept explaining.

"I just want you to understand that you mustn't assume that worth is necessarily determined by who knows you or where you're listed."

Dad gave me one of his I-really-want-you-to-understand looks. "Or that being listed in an encyclopedia means that you are of exclusive and extraordinary worth."

I understood what Dad was saying, but he still hadn't answered the question I had asked in the first place. "So how do you know about Miss Nickerson?" I asked him.

"Miss Nickerson is from Louisiana," Dad said. His serious look melted into a smile. Dad just loooooves to talk about Louisiana because that's where he's from.

"And so, you know her, right?" This was great! I imagined the look on Edna's face when I told her.

"Hold on, baby," Daddy said. "I don't exactly know her— that is, I know *of* her. She comes from a family that's well known. Especially by people in Louisiana, and certainly by musicians."

"Why?"

"Well, one reason is because both her mother and father were outstanding musicians. They started the Nickerson School of Music in New Orleans."

Daddy rubbed the spot on his head that's beginning to get bald. "Camille taught there for a while, I believe."

"She *taught* music when she was a kid?" I was beginning to understand why this Camille Nickerson was something else. "People who wrote reference books must be nuts not to include her."

Dad laughed. "Not when she was a kid," he said. "She taught there after she had graduated from Juilliard, one of the top music schools in this country."

"So what did she do to make her famous?"

"I'm not sure I'd use the word *famous* to describe Camille Nickerson," Dad said. " 'Well known' would be a better term, I think."

"So what did she do to make herself well known?" It was getting harder to know what to think about this Camille Nickerson person.

"Besides being a wonderful musician and an excellent teacher, Camille Nickerson collected the songs of her childhood. African Creole songs that may have been forgotten and lost forever if she hadn't had them published."

"What kind of songs?" I had never heard of the songs Dad was talking about. And I bet nobody else at Miss Elder's had either.

"Songs built on the African and Creole roots of people like the Nickersons. People all over Louisiana," Dad said.

He put his arm around me. "People like me," he said. "And like you."

I didn't know why Dad had such a big smile on his face, but it was so big I could feel it. I could even feel it coming on my face. Weird.

Then Dad had snapped his fingers. Like you do when you remember something you thought you had forgotten and are glad to remember that you didn't forget.

"I think we're in luck, young lady," he said.

Dad started searching through some of his lawyer books.

"Is there something about Miss Nickerson in your books?"

Maybe she'd been in jail or something. That would *really* be something to tell Edna.

"Not about her. *By* her."

Dad pulled out some crumpled-up papers from one of the books. "I can't believe this is still here after all these years," he said. He was grinning like he had found something really special.

"What is it?" I pulled Dad's arm down so I could see what was in his hand.

"This," Dad said, smoothing out the papers. They were sheets of music.

"I remember picking this up years ago," Dad said. "I ran across it in a store when I was home visiting your grand-parents and thought it would be a good thing to keep."

Dad kept smoothing out the wrinkled-up music. He was rubbing his hand across it like he rubs his hand across my back sometimes when he comes in to say good night.

"This is 'Mister Banjo,' a song composed by Camille Nickerson."

Dad gave me the music so I could look at it. I was real careful with it because I could tell it meant a lot to my dad.

We looked at the music together. Dad even started hum-ming some of it. It didn't look like it was hard. Well, not *too* hard, anyhow. That's when I got the idea.

"Dad!" I said. My great idea was getting me excited. "Dad, this would be a super-good piece for the contest!"

Dad got a puzzled look on his face. "You know," I said, "Miss Elder's competition. What I was telling you about in the first place."

"You can play anything you want for the competition?"

"Yep. Miss Elder said she would leave the choice of what to play up to us."

"Amanda, I don't think you could make a better choice," Dad said. He put the music up on the piano. "By playing this piece you'll be doing something the reference books aren't doing. You'll be spreading the word. Telling about the worth of Miss Nickerson."

And I'll be playing something better than anybody else in the competition will ever even DREAM of. Something that's sure to make Miss Nickerson choose me!

I gave my dad a big hug. "Thanks, Dad!" I said. "I sure am glad you told me about Camille Nickerson."

"Mister Banjo" was harder than I thought, but that didn't matter. I was going to memorize it and play it perfectly no matter what. That's the reason I had been working so hard and practicing every single day. I was going to win that competition.

Just wait, Fatso Ernestine. You'll see.

That night Edna called to talk about our shopping trip. I had been holding on to my IOU. I had stuck it in the corner of the mirror on my dresser, and every time I saw that bright red card I remembered I had something special to look forward to.

Edna asked about us going shopping almost every day even though the recital was months away. Sometimes it really got on my nerves, but mostly I didn't mind.

"Have you decided what kind of dress you want?" she asked.

"I only know that I want it to be yellow," I said. "And beautiful. What kind do you want?"

"I haven't even decided what color I want. When I asked Mommy what color she thought I should get, she said I should be worried about what I was going to play, not what I was going to wear."

I didn't ask Edna anything about playing because I didn't want her to ask me. But she did anyway.

"Do you know what you're gonna play?" she said.

"I've been thinkin' about it." It wasn't a lie to say that. "Has Alicia decided?"

"I dunno. I heard her talkin' to Ernestine about the contest the other day, but I didn't hear her say anything about what she was going to play.

Ernestine? Ernestine at Alicia's house?

"Was Ernes—, ah, Fatso over at your house?" I asked. I started coughing.

"Naw. She and Alicia were talking on the phone. They don't ever visit each other. They only talk on the phone. And the contest is all I hear them talkin' about. Every time they talk on the phone."

That's why Alicia is getting so chummy with Ernestine. She wants to make sure she knows what Fatso's going to do for the contest.

"Sometimes your temperamental sister is smarter than we think," I said. My coughing stopped.

"Whatta you talkin' about, Amanda?" Edna said. I could tell she was sorta interested and sorta not.

"Oh, nothing," I said. Alicia wasn't telling what she was up to, and I wasn't either. Maybe that's the way it's supposed to be with sometimes-best friends.

March

13 🐟 Ernestine

THE WIND ALMOST blew me off the sidewalk while I walked to Miss Elder's. I could tell it was almost blowing Alicia away, too. She was coming from the opposite direction. We got to Miss Elder's door at the same time. We stayed outside talking for a little while since we figured we couldn't when we went in. But when we went in, we didn't see Dragon Breath anywhere. What a surprise!

"I wonder where old Dragon Breath is?" Alicia said.

"I'm gonna tell you like my uncle J. B. tells me: 'Don't talk trouble up; it'll find you soon enough.'"

A lot more kids than usual were waiting in the hall. Kids who weren't there on a normal lesson day. Like Merry Lou. I think mostly everybody was waiting around just to listen. To see whose playing was probably going to win the competition.

Carmella Mitchell and Merry Lou were talking to each

other and not even trying to whisper. Something was definitely strange. Alicia asked Carmella what was going on.

"Where's Dra—, I mean, where's Mrs. Elder?" she said.

Carmella didn't even have a chance to answer. Big-mouth Merry Lou butted right in. "Mrs. Elder's not here today. She outta town," she said in her high, whiny voice.

"Is she really, Carmella?" Alicia said, ignoring Merry Lou.

But of course Merry Lou acted like she hadn't even noticed she was being ignored. "She really is," she said. "I know 'cause Uncle Harry took her to the train station. Mrs. Elder went to see her sister who lives—"

Alicia cut Merry Lou off right in the middle of her gossipy sentence. "Thanks, Carmella," she said. "Let's sit over here, Ernestine."

It sure seemed noisy in the waiting hall. Alicia said it probably wasn't all that noisy, but that we were so used to no noise at all, even a little noise seemed like a lot. Neither one of us cared, though. We started laughing and talking like everybody else. I told Alicia about the science project Clovis and I were working on.

"I hope I get to meet Clovis soon. He sounds nice," Alicia said.

"Clovis and I have been friends forever. He's my... I know you'll like each other."

I was about to say that Clovis was my best friend, but I decided to keep that to myself. I knew Alicia and Clovis would like each other and probably become friends themselves. I had already told Alicia that her father was Clovis's dentist, but she still didn't know him.

"Ernestine, I really want to ask you something. And I

want you to know that you don't have to tell me the answer if you don't want to." Alicia's big round eyes looked so serious.

She's going to ask me why I haven't gone on a diet. Why I'm still so fat, even with the contest coming up.

My stomach felt like it was tossing around. "What do you want to know?" I said. I didn't look in her face.

Alicia leaned closer. "A lot of people…" Her voice had gotten real soft.

Here it comes.

"…won't tell what they're going to play for the contest," she said, almost whispering. "I think that's silly. What do you think?"

The tossing stopped. "I think so, too," I said, biting on my tongue to stop the stupid grin that I felt crawling to my face. "I think keeping it a secret is silly, too."

"So, if I tell you what I'm gonna play, will you tell me?"

"Sure."

"So what are you playing?" Alicia said.

"You said you'd go first, " I said. Then we both laughed.

"I'm playing 'Dance Juba.' It's by Nathaniel Dett. I had never heard of it, but Mommy told me about it. She even had a copy of it because she used to play it when she took piano lessons."

"Me, too," I said.

Alicia's eyes got so big I thought they might pop out of her head. I started explaining fast.

"I don't mean I'm playing that piece. I mean I'm playing something that my mama played when she was a little girl. And she said it's still her favorite piece to this day."

"What is it?"

"It's a piece you've probably heard a million times, but Mama said it's a song that brings peace to the soul and that—"

"Ernestine!" Alicia caught hold of my arm. "Will you pllleeeease stop going on and just tell me what it is?"

I had been going on, I guess, so I blurted it out. "I'm gonna play 'Steal Away.' It's a Spiritual."

"Oh, Ernestine. I *have* heard that piece, and it's beautiful." Alicia sounded so happy. So happy that I kept on telling her about my piece.

"Mama said that her mama—my grandma—used to sing that song to her and that listening to it was how she learned to play it and that she used to sing it to me when I was a baby. I don't remember her singing it to me, but I remember hearing it in church practically forever."

It was like I couldn't stop talking.

"And Mama said she was proud that I was going to play 'Steal Away' because it's a song created by black people—"

Alicia grabbed my arm again. "That's exactly what *my* mother said," she said. Her big eyes opened even wider.

This was amazing. "Your mama said that about me playing 'Steal Away'?" I said.

"Not about *you*," Alicia said, laughing. "About *me!* Mommy said she was proud I was playing something composed by a black man. Nathaniel Dett was a black man."

Ever since we had started becoming friends, Alicia and I were finding out that we did a lot of things alike and felt the same way about a lot, too. Whenever we started talking and found this out, we would get quiet for a minute. Kinda like enjoying being quiet inside and knowing that the other person was doing the same thing. That's what Alicia and I were doing when the door to the hall opened and Alicia's sister, Edna, and Miss Stuck-up Amanda walked in.

Edna looked regular—like she always did when I saw her. But Amanda looked even *more* evil than she usually did. And that's evil! But after she opened her mouth, we *really* found out what evil was.

"Hi, everybody in here except two people."

When Amanda said that, she and Edna were practically in my face. Walking in front of me and Alicia. It was the evilest thing I had ever heard. And almost everybody started laughing!

I was ready to pop up out of my chair and give that stuck-up witch a piece of my mind. But Alicia must have been reading my mind, because she put her hand on my arm and held it real tight. She leaned her face so close to mine I could smell her lemon soap.

"Do you care what Amanda says?" Alicia whispered.

"Naw," I said, half trying to whisper and half trying not to. I was trying not to be mad either, but I wasn't getting that half right.

"And you know what I think?" Alicia kept on whispering.

"What?"

"I think Amanda Nelson Clay is afraid that she won't even come close in that contest."

"You think that's her problem?" Now I was whispering, too.

"Don't you?"

"Nope," I said. Then I got close to Alicia's lemon ear.

"I think she's jealous 'cause you and I are friends. That's what I think."

Both Alicia and I sat back in our chairs. Neither one of us said anything, but I was pretty sure she and I were thinking the same thing.

I could tell without even turning my head that Stuck-up Amanda was looking at us. I could hear her talking and laughing with Edna and Brenda Wilson, but I knew she was watching us, too. Then Alicia reached over for my arm again. This time she started hitting on it.

"I have a great idea," she said. Her big eyes got giant wide. "It's a terrific idea and you have to agree to it."

"What is it?"

"Promise first."

"Alicia—"

"Come on, Ernestine, promise. I wouldn't ask you to do something terrible, would I?"

"Shucks," I said. "I was hoping you were thinking about something terrible for You-Know-Who." I laughed.

"Well," Alicia said, laughing too, "maybe it won't be so unterrible for You-Know-Who."

"Tell me, tell me!" Now I was the one who leaned close.

"Well, you know about the Jabberwock, right?"

"Yeah. Mama's busy as a squirrel gettin' ready for it," I said.

"Mommy's like a squirrel, too. Only she's gettin' ready for the party we're having *after* the Jabberwock." Alicia wiggled around in her seat. Whatever she was thinking about was making her more excited while she talked.

"Ernestine," she said, "let's go to the Jabberwock together. Your dad and mom are in it, but only my dad is. We can sit with Mommy. After the Jabberwock I want to you come over to spend the night. Then you can be at the party, too!"

I didn't know what to say. Sleep over at Alicia's? At Dr. Raymond's house? What would Clovis say about that!

"C'mon, Ernestine. Say yes."

"Will You-Know-Who be there?" I asked.

Alicia's wide eyes were almost dancing out of their eyeholes. "I know she'll be coming to the party," she said. "And Edna might invite her to spend the night."

"Then I'll be there, too," I said "Like you said, we'll have a terrific time!"

It felt like my eyes were dancing, too.

April

14 ✒ Amanda

IT WAS SO MUCH fun on my shopping trip! Mother let
Edna and me try on a billion dresses and didn't yell at us
once about making up our minds. She didn't even mind that
we both ordered two desserts at lunch. When we got back
home I thought she would say that it was time for Edna to
go home, but when we asked her if we could try on the
dresses we bought, she said okay.

Madelyn's room was the perfect place for trying on.
She has a full-length mirror that matches her furniture.
While we climbed the stairs, I kept my fingers crossed that
Madelyn would be out.

"Hallelujah!" I said after I opened the door. "Madelyn's
not here. C'mon in, Edna."

I shut the door behind us. I hoped Madelyn would be out
for a while because I would never be able to convince her that
Edna and I were in her room to look at ourselves in her mirror

and *not* through her stuff. Her boring stuff. I knew because I had looked through it lots of times when she wasn't there.

"Oooo, look at these," Edna said. She was looking at Madelyn's pictures. The ones Madelyn had plastered all around the mirror over her dresser.

"Mother told Madelyn she'd better not mess up her walls with taped-up pictures, so Madelyn puts all her mushy photographs on the mirror. Pretty soon there's not gonna be any room left for her to look at herself."

"Madelyn looks good in these pictures," Edna said, examining every picture. "So does Marcus. They go good together."

Most of the time I don't even think about Alicia much anymore. My ex-best friend. Usually when I do, I get so mad I could spit. But sometimes it's hard not to think of her. Like when Edna said that about Madelyn and Fatso's brother. Alicia would never have said something that dumb. Especially not to me.

I decided to ignore what Edna had said. "Let's try on our dresses," I said. "We'd better hurry up before Madelyn comes back."

We put the boxes on Madelyn's bed and pulled out our dresses. Both were long, of course. Edna's was green with lace around the sleeves and the hem. Mine was yellow with a velvet sash and a large rhinestone button at the back. Mine was also prettier, but I didn't say anything about that to Edna.

Edna held up her dress and looked at herself in the mirror. She held up one side of the dress like you do when you're getting ready to curtsy or something, and twirled around and around.

"Aren't you going to try it on?" I asked. That was the reason we had come up to Madelyn's room in the first place.

"We already did. In the store," Edna said, still twirling.
"Anyhow, I don't want to mess my hair up again."

"Then why were you so anxious to bring the dress up
here and look in Madelyn's mirror?"

"I wanted to see myself," she said. "I don't have to try it
on again to know how I'll look in it," she said. "I can tell by
just doing this."

Edna got real close to the mirror. So close that I thought
she would get her nose print on it. Her breath prints did get
on it when she talked.

"You know what's the best thing about this dress,
Amanda?" she said, almost kissing herself in the mirror.

"What?"

"It's nothing like Alicia's dress. Nothing at all."

Since Edna and Alicia are twins, they have a lot of
clothes that are alike. When they were little, Mrs. Raymond
dressed them alike all the time, which was weird because
Edna and Alicia don't look like twins at all.

Alicia looks a lot like their mother and Madelyn says
Edna is the spitting image of their father. My mother says
Edna is going to be the best-looking one when they are
grown. I don't know how she knows that, but right now
Alicia definitely is prettier.

When Brenda Wilson first met Edna and Alicia she
couldn't believe they were twins. "Y'all don't look nothin'
alike," she said. She also talked about Alicia's long, pretty
hair right in front of Edna, who's always fussing about her
hair, which is a lot shorter. After Brenda walked away, Alicia

told Edna how nice her hair always looked and how just be-cause Brenda could play the piano well it didn't mean she was all that smart about other things.

That's the way Alicia used to be all the time. Nice. Sweet. And smart. Not anymore. Not since she started being so tight with Fatso.

I was beginning to feel like I wanted to spit. I stopped thinking about Alicia and decided I wouldn't think about her anymore.

"Amanda," Edna said. She was still pressed up against the mirror. "What are you wearing to the Jabberwock?"

"I dunno. What are you wearing?"

"I dunno know either, but Mommy said that maybe Alicia and me should wear something purple and gold be-cause those are the colors of Daddy's fraternity. Omega Psi Phi."

Sometimes adults are really stupid. I said, "If you wore any special color, wouldn't it be better to wear the colors of your mom's sorority?"

"Mommy's not in a sorority, remember?"

I had forgotten. And I should have remembered because I knew that Edna and I (and probably the temperamental one also) would be sitting with Mrs. Raymond at the Jabberwock. She was the only parent who wasn't a Greek. (It always sounded so weird to hear our parents call them-selves that when they meant belonging to a sorority or fra-ternity.) My mother and dad and all the other Greeks were going to be in the Jabberwock and not the audience.

Edna finally moved away from the mirror. She started folding up her dress.

"Oh, yeah," Edna said, "there's something I have to tell you."

"What?" I was holding up my dress getting ready to put it on a hanger.

"Guess who's going with us to the Jabberwock and is going to be at the party *and* is spending the night."

I hate guessing and Edna knows it. So I just waited.

"Ernestine."

I couldn't believe what I was hearing. I dropped my brand-new beautiful dress on the floor.

"WHAT?"

"Yep. Fatso Ernestine is gonna be sleeping over."

Edna didn't look mad at all, like she should have. In fact, she almost looked like she was about to smile.

"Don't you mind?" I picked up my dress, but still couldn't believe what she had said.

"Yeah, I mind, but what can I do? Mommy said each of us could invite one person over. Alicia invited Ernestine, and I invited you."

Alicia invited Ernestine! She invited Ernestine and not ME!

I almost accidentally pulled the rhinestone button off the back of the dress when I tried to unfasten it so I could put it on a hanger. I spread the dress across Madelyn's bed instead. I'd hang it up later.

I sat down beside my dress and started smoothing it out. "How long ago did she invite her?" I said.

I didn't look at Edna. She wasn't looking at me either. She was wrapping the tissue paper from the box around her dress.

"Ernestine's the reason Mommy said each of us could invite someone over to spend the night," she said. "After Alicia told Mommy she had invited Ernestine, I invited you."

Alicia didn't even think about inviting me. She only wanted to invite Ernestine. Fatso Ernestine.

"Has Ernestine ever been to your house before?"

"Nope. But Alicia's been to her house."

"She *has?*" I couldn't believe all of this.

"She went over there last Saturday and had lunch with Fatso and one of her friends. Somebody named Clovis. No big deal," Edna said. She was having trouble fastening her box.

I reached over to help her. "I didn't say it was a big deal. I'm just surprised, that's all. And you never said anything about her going over there."

"So what if Alicia goes to Fatso's house. Who cares," Edna said. "We'll ignore the two of them on the night of the Jabber-wock just like we do all the time, right?"

"Right."

All of this was beginning to get on my nerves. And from the way she had settled down on Madelyn's bed, it didn't look like Edna would be ready to go home anytime soon.

Maybe I should tell her that I have a headache. I think I am beginning to get one. I won't be lying if I say I feel bad.

"Edna, I—"

I didn't get a chance to finish. The Voices that had been only little rumbles downstairs got louder all of a sudden. Much, much louder.

"George, I can't take much more of this. I just can't."

"*You* can't take much more? What about me?"

"What do you have to take, George? I'd love to know. I *need* to know what the great, duplicitous George Carver

Clay, Esquire, has to take. Please tell me."

I looked at Edna. She was looking at me so I knew I had to say something. It was time to finish what I was going to say in the first place.

"Edna, I—"

I didn't get to finish again. This time Edna interrupted me.

"Amanda, I almost forgot," she said. "It's my turn to help fix dinner. I'd better go right away or I'm gonna get in trouble."

We made a ton of noise coming down the stairs. By the time we got to the front door, Mother and Dad weren't around. Neither were their Voices.

"Thank your mom for the great shopping trip," Edna said. "I'll tell her myself tomorrow, but now I better get home."

"I'll tell her," I said. "See you later."

Just before I closed the door all the way, Edna turned around and came back. "Amanda," she said, "parents are weird, but they can work things out. Just wait. You'll see." Then she ran across the yard to her house.

Edna. My new best friend.

15 🐾 *Ernestine*

GOING TO THE Jabberwock was exciting enough, but when we got there and the usher led us to box seats, I thought I would bust!

After we all got seated, I turned around to whisper to Alicia's mother, "Mrs. Raymond, these seats are wonderful!"

"I'm enjoying them too, Ernestine," she whispered back and smiled at me. When Mrs. Raymond smiled, she looked exactly like Alicia.

I had been in the Memorial Building before to go to concerts and plays and stuff like that, but I always sat in one of the joined-together seats on the main floor or in the balcony. I had never even been in one of the boxes before. And now I was *sitting* in one.

There are twelve boxes in the Memorial Building, six on each side. The seats are above the main floor but below the balcony. Each box has eight red velvet chairs you can move around any way you want. You can't do that with the joined-together seats.

No matter where the box is, box seats are the best ones to have. Our box was on the left side and the second one from the stage. The view was so good I could see the Xs they had taped down on the stage, even though the tape was almost the same color as the stage floor. Mrs. Raymond said the Xs were marks for the performers to help them know where to stand.

From the box it was easy to see all of my friends. What's even better, they could see me! When Jazz came in with her godmother, I wanted to stick my tongue out at her. I didn't though. When she looked up at us, I just waved and did one of *her* kind of smiles.

You could see so much from our box that I practically forgot that Miss Stuck-up was in there, too. Mrs. Raymond had told the four of us to sit on the front row of chairs. She and her friend Mrs. Hughes sat in the second row. (There were even two seats left over!) I sat in the first seat, Alicia in the second, Edna in the third, and Real Pain Amanda sat in the fourth. Every time I turned my head to the right I would remember that she was there. After a while I figured out that I should keep my eyes on the stage. So that's what I did.

We had our own little ceiling light in our box. When it was time for the show to start, the box lights didn't go all the way off like the lights in the big ceiling over the whole auditorium. The little box lights just dimmed.

I'm always excited when it's time for a show to get started. Not a movie show; a show with real people in it. That night I was more excited than ever. Mostly because Mama and

Daddy were going to be in the show, but also because I was going to be able to see a show better than ever before. When our little ceiling light dimmed, it was hard for me to keep from grinning.

Everybody clapped when the Lawson Brothers came out on the stage, all of them dressed in tuxedos. Everybody I know loves to hear the Lawsons play. Mr. Lawson—he's actually the father—plays the piano, Chauncy plays the violin, Davis plays the cello, and Martin plays the clarinet. Martin is just a little older than me and he already plays as good as the rest of his family.

Mr. Lawson came up to the microphone while the rest of them sat in chairs placed around the piano. "Good evening, Ladies and Gentlemen," he said. "Let us stand for 'Lift Every Voice and Sing.'"

I leaned over to whisper in Alicia's ear. "All the Lawsons go to my church," I said. "That's where they all learned how to play music."

"Who's the one playing the clarinet?" Alicia whispered to me.

"That's Martin," I whispered back. "He's just a little older than us."

"He's cute," Alicia said. We both started laughing.

Mrs. Raymond tapped Alicia on her shoulder. "Shhh," she said.

I could see Evil Eyes looking at us. She was probably hoping we'd get in trouble. I stopped laughing right away. Anyhow, the music was starting.

The words to "Lift Every Voice and Sing" were printed on the back of the program so everybody could sing along. I didn't need to look, though, because I've known all the words practically forever.

Lift every voice and sing
Till earth and heaven ring,
Ring with the harmonies of Liberty;
Let our rejoicing rise
High as the listening skies,
Let it resound loud as the rolling sea.

I could hear Mrs. Raymond and Mrs. Hughes singing behind me. Their voices sounded pretty. All the voices and the music sounded so good that when it got to my favorite part I felt like singing as hard as I could. The kind of singing Daddy calls "serenading with your heart."

Sing a song full of the faith that the dark past has taught us,
Sing a song full of the hope that the present has brought us.

Alicia must have felt the same way because she started serenading with her heart too.

Facing the rising sun of our new day begun
Let us march on till victory is won.

At the end we all clapped like crazy. Partly for the Lawsons, but mostly for ourselves, I think. The clapping didn't stop until Mrs. Taylor came on the stage to give the welcome.

Mrs. Taylor had been over at our house a lot lately. *Too* much for me and Jazz. Mama told us that she and Mrs. Taylor were working together on the Jabberwock since Mrs. Taylor was the president of the Deltas that year and Mama was head of the Jabberwock committee.

Mrs. Taylor's face is really, really thin, and she has a voice that goes up high and then low while she talks. A singsongy voice. At first Jazz and I thought her voice was what made her face look strange. But then Jazz figured out that wasn't it. The strange thing is how it looks like some invisible hands are holding her cheeks together and pushing everything on her face to the middle.

I tried very, very hard not to think about this as I watched Mrs. Taylor give her speech.

> Ladies and Gentlemen, on behalf of Delta Sigma Theta, welcome to our fifteenth annual Jabberwock. This event is a Delta tradition and gives us an opportunity to come together, share our talents, have fun, and win prizes.
>
> The Jabberwock has been a Delta affair since nineteen twenty-five. It's a way of raising money for our scholarship fund—a fund that will help educate the true wealth of our community: our young people. The Jabberwock also lets us Greeks come together on friendly terms to show off for each other—and at the same time show each other up!

The audience started laughing when Mrs. Taylor said that. Alicia saw me laughing, too, so she leaned over and asked, "What did she say that was funny?" With everybody laughing so much she didn't even have to whisper.

I didn't know what had been so funny either. But I had been wanting to laugh ever since Miss Pushed-together Face with the Go-Up-Go-Down voice had come on the stage. When everybody else started laughing, I could finally let mine pop out.

Before I answered Alicia, I used my hands to push in my face from both sides. Then I turned to look at Alicia and answered in my best singsongy voice, "They're just laughing at me, I guess. Poor pinchy-face me."

Alicia started laughing so hard, I thought she was going to fall out of her chair. Edna started laughing, too. But the real surprise was who else laughed: Amanda!

I could tell she was looking in my direction even before I turned around with my Taylor-face, but I figured she'd just glare at me like she always does. When she started laughing with Alicia and Edna, I almost fell out of *my* chair!

Amanda's laugh didn't pop out like laughs usually do. The way her laugh came out reminded me of water in Mama's tea kettle. When you fill the kettle too full of water and then turn up the gas, the kettle screams instead of whistles when the water starts boiling. And the extra water bubbles up and spills out onto the stove.

I wonder if there's something extra in Amanda that makes her laugh like that...

I don't think any of us heard the rest of Mrs. Taylor's speech. We all kept our heads down because every time we looked on the stage, one of us would start laughing and the rest would do the same thing. We didn't want Mrs. Raymond to have to tell us to be quiet, but it got harder and harder not to laugh.

Maybe this night will be more fun than I ever thought!

16 *Amanda*

THERE WAS SO MUCH party noise in the Raymonds' house I couldn't believe it. I almost couldn't hear myself think! And I definitely couldn't hear what Mrs. Raymond was saying, and she was standing right next to me in the crowded basement.

"What did you say?" I moved closer to Mrs. Raymond. Then she bent over and spoke right in my ear.

"I said I hope you girls are having a nice time together. Are you?"

"A terrific time," I said. "This is a great party."

I thought how Mrs. Raymond was being very sweet. I've been coming over to their house and having fun there almost my whole life, and she still was taking time to ask me if I was having a nice time. I also thought that it was too bad Alicia's not more like her mother.

Maybe she thought we wouldn't be having fun because

there were so many adults at the party and almost no kids. A ton of people had come, mostly the people who had been in the Jabberwock and their husbands or wives. Besides me and Edna and Alicia and Alicia's special guest, the only other kids were Tammy and Jason Price, and they were both asleep in Dr. and Mrs. Raymond's bedroom. Besides they were only four and six.

It was still a great party. Even having Fatso there didn't bother me too much, mostly because I didn't have to be with her. People were everywhere in the house, but most of the party was in the Raymonds' basement, where there's a record player and people can dance.

One thing that was fun was seeing all the adults dancing and clowning. Stuff like Dr. Raymond was doing when he came over and started teasing me.

"Come on, my pretty young lady," he said. He held out his hand to me like he was asking me to dance. "Let's trip the light fantastic."

Because of all the noise, I knew I hadn't heard Dr. Raymond right. It sounded like he said we should trip somebody. "Let's trip *who?*" I asked.

Dr. Raymond laughed like I had said something really funny. "Watch it, Amanda," he said. "You're making me remember how old I'm getting." Then he started twirling me around and around like we were dancing.

"Are you girls having fun?" he asked.

I couldn't believe how much the Raymonds were worrying about how much fun everybody was having. It was almost weird.

"Yep," I said. "We're having lots of fun."

"Great!" he said. "I'm glad everyone's getting along."

Edna came over to us. When she did, Dr. Raymond pretended to kiss our hands, and then left.

Edna said something, but I couldn't tell what it was. "What?" I said. I was almost hollering.

"I said, LET'S GO UPSTAIRS. IT'S TOO NOISY DOWN HERE!" She *did* holler.

"WHAT DID YOU DO THAT FOR?" I said, hollering back at her.

"BECAUSE THAT'S THE ONLY WAY WE CAN HEAR EACH OTHER," Edna said. She was giggling like crazy.

I laughed, too. Both of us were standing there almost yelling our heads off, and nobody was telling us to shut up. Nobody acted like they even noticed!

"C'MON, FOLLOW ME," Edna said. She said it a lot louder than she had to. That made it even funnier. Both of us ran up the basement steps, laughing so hard we almost fell *up* the stairs.

"Where's Alicia and Ernestine?" Edna asked when we got to the kitchen.

I half wanted to say I didn't know where Fatso and her temperamental friend were, but I didn't. I hadn't called either of them names all night. I hadn't called them period.

"Ummmmm!" Edna had opened the refrigerator door and was looking at the trays of fancy sandwiches and pickles and olives and other party stuff. The bread sandwiches were cut into little shapes like diamonds and hearts and stars. There were cracker sandwiches, too, with pieces of cheese or shrimp or tomato on top. Some of the little sandwiches had stacks of things on them held together with a toothpick.

"Let's pick out a tray to take upstairs for ourselves,"

"Won't your mother get mad?"

"Nope," Edna said, reaching for the tray that had a lot of red and yellow on it. "What about this one?" she said.

"Why won't she get mad?" I knew Mrs. Raymond let her kids get away with a lot, but even she would get mad if Edna took away one of the trays made especially for the party.

"Because," she said, poking around on the tray with her fingers. Edna acted like she didn't have any idea about what I was talking about.

"Because WHAT?" I asked.

She looked at me like *I* was weird, then words started coming out her mouth so fast they almost mooshed together.

"Because Mommy said that you and me and Ernestine and Alicia could have our own tray of sandwiches and that we could take it up to our room with some pop if we wanted to and that all of us—me and Alicia *and* you and Ernestine—should share the refreshments and get along and enjoy ourselves like civilized young ladies."

I stood there looking at Edna. I was about to ask her what her problem was when something fell right into my brain. Something that let me know that the weird way Dr. and Mrs. Raymond—and even Edna!—had been acting wasn't so weird after all. And it was all Alicia's fault. My *EX*-best friend.

Alicia had probably been talking to her mother and father about how I didn't like her precious Ernestine. I bet she had even told Mrs. Raymond that I called Ernestine "Fatso" sometimes.

That was really dirty. I had never called Ernestine by that name to her face. But what if I had? It wasn't Alicia's business what I called anybody. And I could *not* like anybody I wanted to. Especially somebody who acted like she didn't like me one bit either.

Alicia was probably trying to turn her whole family against me. Even Edna, I bet!

"What's wrong with it?"

I had been standing there looking right in Edna's face, but I hadn't heard anything she had said. "What's wrong with what?" I asked.

"What's wrong with this tray of sandwiches?" she said.

"Who said something was wrong with it?" I answered.

"I keep asking you if you think it's okay, and all you do is stand there with this mean look on your face."

Just like I thought! Alicia *was* trying to turn all the Raymonds against me.

I started helping Edna take the paper off the tray she had chosen. "I think this tray looks great, Edna," I said. "And I wasn't even thinking about the food at all. I was thinking how sorry I am that Dad's fraternity didn't win the Jabberwock. That was probably the look you saw."

"Then it's okay with you if you and me and Ernestine and Alicia eat this together?" Edna said.

"That'll be great," I said. "You get the pop, and I'll get four glasses and some ice."

Just wait, Alicia. I'll show you. You're not gonna know anybody any nicer than me. Just wait. You'll see.

Fat—uh, I mean, Ernestine and Alicia were in the living room looking at Dr. Raymond's African stuff. The statues and masks that are on the tables and walls. One of the statues is so big that it sits on the floor behind the couch. It's really weird.

Alicia was telling her new best friend about her dad's collection. "Daddy says that when me and Edna inherit these, they'll be worth a fortune."

"They're so beautiful," Ernestine said. It sounded like she really meant it. That girl couldn't *not* be strange if she tried.

"Do you really think so?" Edna said, holding on to the big tray of sandwiches.

"They're *wonderful!*" Ernestine said. Her eyes were glued to the big floor statue. "Don't you think so?"

"I guess," Edna said. "Anyhow Daddy says they are, so they probably are. All I know is what they're good for."

The shape of the big statue makes it look like it has a shelf on one side. Edna put her tray on this part.

"You'd better get that offa there, girl!" Alicia acted like she was about to have a fit. "You're gonna break it."

"What's the matter with you?" Edna still had her hands on the tray but she hadn't moved it one bit off the statue. "*You* don't think it's all that wonderful."

A smile was all over Edna's face. Even in her eyes. I knew she wanted me to laugh with her, but I wasn't going to.

Give Alicia something else to tell her parents about? Not me.

Alicia was about ready to yell at Edna again when Edna took the tray off the statue. Finally. She put it down on the table next to the couch. That was where I had already put the pop and ice and stuff I had been carrying.

Alicia looked at Ernestine. "Do you want to see the other big statue?" she said.

Ernestine nodded her head, so Alicia led the way into the dining room. I decided to follow them, and Edna followed me.

The light was off in the dining room. When Alicia reached to turn it on, Ernestine made a sound like somebody was choking her. It almost scared us to death. Then she grabbed Alicia's arm and said, "Hold on!"

We all looked at Ernestine. She had one hand on Alicia's arm and her other hand pointing at the window. Our eyes followed the pointing finger like we were in a dream trance or something. Then we saw what she had seen.

Two people were standing out in the yard, and they were kissing! The kind of Oh-Darling-I-love-you-so-much kissing like you see in the movies. They were really in a clinch.

We all started giggling like crazy. We couldn't help ourselves. It was sooooo weird to see them. Ernestine kept saying "Shhhh," while we walked closer to the window to get a better look, but all of us kept laughing.

I think I saw who it was first, but Ernestine said later that she did. It's hard to tell because both of us screamed at the same time. And we screamed almost the exact same thing.

"Oh no! It's…!"

Ernestine screamed "Marcus" and I screamed "Madelyn." And it *was* Madelyn and Marcus right outside the Raymonds' dining-room window. Madelyn and Marcus in a big love clinch.

Then the weirdest thing of all happened. I just couldn't believe it. Ernestine and I said the same thing again. Only this time it was the all-the-way EXACT thing.

"I'm gonna tell!"

Ernestine and I looked at each other. I saw how I felt on her face. I think she saw how she felt on mine. I wanted to say something, but I didn't know what to say. The only thing I felt like doing was laughing. So that's what I did.

And that's exactly what Ernestine did, too. She laughed. Both of us stood there laughing and laughing. Right there in the dining room, in the dark, beside the second big African floor statue that Dr. Raymond called one of his treasures.

May

17 🐦 *Ernestine*

THE CLOCK OUTSIDE the choir room in our church said five minutes before eleven o'clock, exactly when my shoe buckle popped open for the second time. It popped open the first time at exactly ten-thirty. I knew because I had decided to keep my eyes on the clock until it was one minute before eleven, the time I would go out onto the pulpit. I was supposed to walk out and sit at the piano one minute before the choir marched in.

"C'mon, baby, hurry up! It's almost time."

I knew Miss Helen was getting nervous, so I tried to hurry up and finish buckling my shoe. It was a good thing I knew Mama planned on buying me new shoes for the recital because the old ones were wearing out fast. At first I thought it might be my feet getting bigger, but I figure feet don't get fat, and I could see that mine weren't getting any longer.

"You need some help, Ernestine?"

I could almost hear Miss Helen's smile. She always had one on her face when it was time for me to go out and start playing for church, so I knew she'd have one on today. A BIG one.

"No, ma'am," I said. "I'm ready now."

"You got all your music?" Miss Helen patted the little pile of music on the table by the door.

"Yep— I mean, yes, ma'am. I got it all together as soon as I got here," I said, picking up the pile.

The choir people started lining up. The *Adult* Choir. Suddenly I felt like swallowing, but my mouth was practically all-the-way dry.

Miss Helen leaned over next to my face. I could smell the peppermint that's always on her breath on Sunday morning. "You not nervous, are you, baby?" she said.

Behind her glasses, Miss Helen's eyes looked twice as big as usual. Looking at them made me feel twice as brave as usual.

"No, ma'am," I said. And it was the truth.

"Good," she said. Her smile popped out bigger than ever. "Because you gonna be just wonderful out there. You always are, and now you gonna be *double* wonderful, playing for the Adult Choir, and all."

I was wishing that Miss Helen would just look at me with her big marble eyes and *not* remind me that I was getting ready to play for the Adult Choir to sing in church. For the first time ever! I was about ready to ask her to please not say anything else when she patted me on the cheek and put a piece of peppermint in my hand. Then she was gone.

"All right, folks, it's time."

Reverend James's voice made me jump. Back there behind the pulpit, it sounded like a drum.

"Are you ready, Miss Ernestine?" Reverend James said. He was grinning at me just like Miss Helen had been. Even some of the choir members were looking at me the same way. Maybe that was the Adult Choir look for whoever played the piano for them.

"I'm ready," I said. And I was.

Reverend James went through the curtains that lead to the pulpit. I followed him. In addition to being the first time to play for the grown folks choir, this was the first time I would be playing the piano right on the pulpit. The preaching stage. That's what Jazz used to call the pulpit when she was little. I thought about this just as I stepped through the curtains. I tried to stop myself, but I couldn't keep from smiling at what I was thinking.

I'm getting ready to play on the preaching stage. And I'm playing for the Adult Choir!

As soon as I sat down, Reverend James held his arms open and said, "Welcome, Sisters and Brothers. Welcome to the House of the Lord!" His voice sounded like a bell and a drum at the same time.

The organ started, then the drums, and then it was my turn to join in. And I did, without a single mistake!

After the second song, everything felt really good. It was just like Miss Helen had said: it felt like I had been playing for the Adult Choir practically my whole life. Up there on the preaching stage.

I started looking around to see where Jazz was sitting. I knew she wouldn't be sitting with Mama and Daddy and

Marcus where we usually sat every Sunday because she said she was going sit with Regina, and that they were going to sit some place where they could look up and make faces at me.

I was going to beat her to it. I figured I'd be able to make faces at *her* while Reverend James was preaching. Nobody would be watching me then.

That's when I saw Amanda. While I was looking around for Jazz. Amanda was sitting next to Mrs. Vines, who used to teach my Sunday school class. She had been the best Sunday school teacher in the universe. So much fun! Everybody in her class loved her to death. I couldn't figure why she would be with Amanda.

Mrs. Vines was whispering something to Amanda, but Amanda was looking right at me. She wasn't looking evil like she usually does when we're at Miss Elder's, but she wasn't looking exactly smiley either.

Ever since the party on Jabberwock night I had started thinking that Amanda wasn't so awful bad. In fact, there was something about her that I...ah, not really liked, but didn't really hate anymore either. Especially since that night all of us had been at the sleep-over and had talked and stuff until way after the Jabberwock party was over. Both of us even had decided not to tell our parents about what we had seen when we looked out the Raymonds' dining-room window. Still, even if I was surprised to see her at my church, I didn't care much one way or the other.

So I kept on looking around. Maybe Amanda's sister was there, too. Maybe even bunched up next to my brother. That's almost what I expected to see when I got my *big* surprise for the day.

Sitting right behind Jazz was Miss Elder. She was wearing a pretty pink hat with white flowers, and she was sitting next to someone who had on a white hat with pink flowers. Someone I had never seen in person before, but who I knew from her picture: Miss Camille Nickerson. It couldn't have been anybody else!

I couldn't stop the smile from coming on my face. I had told Miss Elder that I was going to be playing for the Adult Choir for the first time. She had even listened to the special song I was going to play for offertory. I hadn't dared to ask her to come. I figured she would be too busy. She had told us that Miss Nickerson would be coming soon because the contest would be on Wednesday and the recital next Sunday. But Miss Elder had come to my church anyway. All on her own. And she had brought her famous friend with her!

One of those smiles-that-won't-go-away stuck on my face. I hoped my dumb sister wouldn't think it was for her, but with her sitting in front of Miss Elder and Miss Nickerson, she was getting the smile, too. And there was no way I was going to stick my tongue out at her like I had planned on doing.

I turned around to the keyboard to get ready for the third song. I felt even better than I had before.

Miss Elder told Miss Nickerson something that made her want to come to my church on the day I would be playing for the Adult Choir. Miss Nickerson was listening to me play the piano!

I wanted to look back at Amanda. But I knew that if I did, the smile-that-wouldn't-go-away might turn into a big, fat laugh!

18 ✐ *Amanda*

GODMOTHER FRANKIE called early that Sunday morning, and I was super glad. I knew she was calling to ask if I wanted to go somewhere with her. Whenever she calls on Sunday morning, she usually wants to make a date. That's what she'll say—"Are you free for a date today, Godchild?"

Godmother Frankie is the wildest person I know. She is so much fun! She's more fun than any grown person I can even imagine. She's even more fun than most of my friends.

But that Sunday morning she was saving my life by calling. I didn't even mind that she wanted to start our date by going to church, even her church, where the services go on for a super-long time. But that didn't matter. Going anywhere away from the house was saving my life.

Godmother Frankie was the one person I wanted to talk to about…well, things, but Madelyn said not to tell anyone about what was going on with Mother and Dad. Anyhow, lately things seemed to be…well, different. I almost never heard the Voices anymore. But when Dad and Mother were both home and in the same room, it was so silent that the *silence* was noisy. Weird.

They were acting different, too. Both of them were being extra nice to us. Like Mother telling me and Madelyn not to worry about doing dinner dishes. That she would do them while we did homework or relaxed or something. And Dad offering to take us for ice cream or to the drive-in. On a school night. That was really weird.

I thought I'd talk to my godmother about it anyway. She'd keep a secret if I asked her to, and then Madelyn wouldn't have to know. I could tell Godmother while we were on our way to church. That way the telling would be over with and I could forget about it for the rest of our date.

I waited for Godmother Frankie outside so she wouldn't have to get out of the car and ring the doorbell for me. While I waited I started practicing what I was going to say. But the pretty sunny sky and nice smelling air made me keep messing up. So I decided to forget it. It might end up ruining my date. Anyhow, I *had* promised Madelyn.

We could hear the music playing even before we went in-side the church. The music is the best part about going to my godmother's church. They have an organ and a piano *and* drums. You sorta feel like rocking to the music no matter if it's fast or slow. It's a lot different from the music in the church my parents and me and Madelyn go to—when we go. The music in that church just makes you want to sleep.

We got to our seats just as it was time for the minister and the choir to come out. I was glad we were in time. The people in the choir sorta rock when they march in, and I really like to see that.

When I saw who came out behind the minister to play the piano, I couldn't believe it! I couldn't believe it so much, I almost rubbed my eyes like people do when they're seeing a miracle. Or a disaster.

Always before when I had seen her playing the piano for church, Ernestine had been down on the regular floor and not up on the pulpit. And *never* with the grown people's choir. But there she was all right, and with a huge grin on her face. I just couldn't believe it!

After the organ and drums started, Ernestine joined in just like she was a part of everything. And I guess she was, because everything sounded pretty okay. But not good enough to make me want to rock like I usually did.

After the music stopped, Godmother Frankie leaned over to ask me if I recognized the girl playing the piano. How she was the same one we had seen playing for the little kids' choir when I had come to church with her before, and how much the girl had "grown as a musician."

I got ready to lean over to whisper to Godmother that I knew Ernestine Harris because she took music lessons from the same teacher as I did. That we weren't really friends or anything like that, but had ended up being together with my friends the Raymond twins on the night of the Jabberwock. That all of us who took lessons from Miss Elder were going to be in her contest with a *lot* of kids who had been practicing really hard and could play the piano good. I had my mouth open to tell my godmother all of that when I saw

Ernestine looking out from the stage with another one of those giant grins on her face. This one was so huge I raised myself up to see who it was for. And then I saw something I super-couldn't believe.

Miss Elder was sitting in the congregation, and Miss *Nickerson* was with her. I recognized Miss Nickerson right away from her picture. And they were *there*, in Godmother Frankie's church, listening to Ernestine play the piano. I just couldn't believe it!

Well, of course Ernestine had invited them! Why else would they come? In the first place, they wouldn't even know about her playing if she hadn't told them. She probably wanted them to see her playing for the big choir so they would think she was super wonderful when they got ready to decide the contest.

Being in the church was beginning to get on my nerves. Then, just as I was about to tell Godmother that I was feeling a little hot, she leaned over to me and whispered, "Amanda, look over there. To your left. The woman sitting next to your piano teacher is Camille Nickerson."

"You know Camille Nickerson?" I was surprised. Godmother Frankie knew about the contest and the recital because she was coming with my parents. But I didn't think she would be able to recognize Miss Nickerson. She was just well known and not even famous.

"How do you know her?" I whispered back.

"Remember, now," Godmother said, winking at me, "I'm a Louisiana lady just like she is."

I had forgotten that Godmother Frankie had come from Louisiana just like my dad. That's how come she's my godmother in the first place. She and my dad have been friends almost their whole lives.

"Do you really know her?" It was getting hard to keep my whisper. "I mean, do you know her well enough to talk to her?"

Godmother Frankie put her finger over her lips and said "Shhhh" real quiet. Then she leaned over and whispered in my ear.

"I know her well enough even to have *you* talk to her. I'll introduce you to her after church."

This was great! Thanks to the best godmother in the world, Ernestine's plan was going to go up in smoke. Miss Nickerson might hear Ernestine play the piano, but *I* was going to meet her in person. *I* was going to talk with her. *I* would be the one she would remember for sure.

I wanted to laugh out loud. Of course I didn't, but when the music started again, I suddenly felt like rocking. So I did.

19 ✒ *Ernestine*

I HAD GONE into Mama's room without making a sound. I wanted privacy while I stood in front of her floor mirror.

"Ernestine, if you only just breath too hard, you gonna bust out that long dress!"

I was so mad to see Jazz standing in the doorway of Mama and Daddy's room that I practically did bust out my dress.

"Get OUTTA here, Jessie Louise!" I yelled. I tried to kick the door shut with my foot.

"You better stop kicking Mama's door," Jazz said. She pushed her behind at the door to keep it from slamming.

"And you better stop pushin' it!" I said. "Anyhow, you're not even suppos' to be in here. Mama said I could be in here by myself to try on my new dress."

"I ain't stoppin' you," she said, putting her hands on her skinny hips.

"Yes, you are." I felt like screaming at Jazz.

"How?" she said, shaking her face at me.

"BY STEALING MY PRIVACY, THAT'S HOW!" This time I didn't stop myself from screaming at her.

"Hey! What's all this fuss out here?"

Marcus came out of the bathroom. I was as surprised to see him as I had been mad to see my pain-in-the-rear sister. I thought Marcus had left the house a long time ago with Daddy.

"What are *you* doing here?" I said. I tried to hide most of myself behind the bedroom door.

"They tell me I live here," Marcus said. "Has something changed? Is there something I should know?"

"You know what I mean, Marcus. You said you were going downtown with Daddy."

Marcus kept on standing there, grinning at me. "Nope," he said.

"Whadda you mean, 'nope'? I heard you tellin' Daddy that you were."

"I said I was *thinking* about going. I didn't say I was," he said. "But why do you care one way or the other?"

"Ernestine don't want nobody to see her bust out her new dress," Jazz said. She still hadn't moved away one single inch.

"Ernestine *doesn't* want *any*body to see her," Marcus said to Jazz. He sounded like Daddy does sometimes when he's trying to get Jazz to talk a certain way.

"I know. That's what I said," Jazz said. She started laughing. She knew what Marcus meant. She was just being Jazz.

Jazz was being Jazz, and Marcus was being Marcus, and both of them were being a real BIG pain. It was time for a new plan.

"C'mon, y'all." I started closing the door. Real slow. "I have to do something in here to get ready for the recital. Cooperate. Please, please, please." I made my voice sound like a scoop of ice cream.

"So, you *did* win the contest!" Marcus stopped the door with his foot. "Ernestine, you're the one who's going to be playing tomorrow with that lady from Louisiana," he said, sounding all happy.

"I didn't say that," I said. I was still trying to push the door shut, and I felt like screaming again. "And her name is Miss Nickerson. Miss Camille Nickerson."

"The only name I care about is yours." Marcus's big foot was still in the door. "That's the name I want to see on the program. Is it gonna be there?"

"I told everybody last night at dinner that we're not gonna tell who won the competition. If you wanna know, come to the recital."

"Will you tell if we promise to go away?" Jazz said. Now she was sitting on the floor of the hallway.

"No, no, NO!"

My sister and brother were being *giant* pains. They were going to torment me forever. It was time for my best plan.

"Marcus, if you don't go away and take Jazz with you, I'm gonna tell you-know-what," I said.

Marcus looked at me like I had started talking in a brand-new language. But not Jazz. She knew tattletale language good.

"Whachu know, Ernestine?" she said. She jumped up from the floor. "Whachu got on Marcus?"

"Yeah, Ernestine," Marcus said. "What do you have on

me?" Marcus sounded like he really didn't know. So I gave him a clue.

"Remember the Jabberwock party?" I said. "Outside on the Raymonds' lawn?"

Mama says all of her children have Morgan eyes. That everybody on her side of the family has big brown eyes. The three of us do too, and Marcus's are the biggest. But after I told him my clue, Marcus's big eyes got so narrow they almost disappeared. His voice got narrow too.

"Whachu you trying to say, Ernestine?" he said. His narrow voice was hard to hear.

Jazz pulled on my arm. "What about the Jabberwock party. What happened on the lawn?" Her eyes were as big as soup bowls.

I figured Marcus would say something then. But he didn't and I didn't either.

Being so nosy, Jazz was about to bust. "What happened?" she said, almost yelling.

Marcus kept looking at me, and I kept looking at him.

"If y'all don't tell, I'm gonna tell Mama," Jazz said.

"What you gonna tell her?" I said. Marcus just stood there still being quiet.

"I'm gonna tell her that…that…that you saw Marcus at the Jabberwock party and that he was outside—"

"And Mama's gonna tell you to mind your own business 'cause that ain't nothin' to tell. Then you gonna be the one gettin' in trouble."

Marcus's eyes stopped being narrow. I was glad because I thought he might keep looking at me like that forever and that I would never see his eyes get big and round again.

"C'mon, Miss Jazz," he said, grabbing hold of her hand. "Let's you and me go on downstairs. I was about ready to fix myself a Marcus burger, and if you help, I'll fix you one too."

Marcus makes the absolute best hamburgers in the world. Even thinking about one makes your mouth water. Jazz must have started thinking about this because she didn't say anything else about telling Mama. She just stuck out her skinny tongue at me and pulled on Marcus's hand.

"And I don't care if you're playing with the Louisiana Lady or not. If you're not playin' with Hazel Scott I don't even want to listen," she said.

I didn't know who Hazel Scott was, but I figured she must be a jazz piano player because that's all my sister listens to.

"Want us to fix you a burger?" Marcus said, looking at me.

A picture of one of those juicy burgers was running across my brain. But my eyes remembered what they had seen in Mama's floor mirror. Me in my dress with one of the snaps on the side already popped open.

"I'm not hungry," I said. "Thanks, anyhow."

"Anything for my sis," Marcus said. He gave me a big, shiny Jazz smile and then went with her down the steps.

Mama says that all the mirrors in our house are members of our family and that they love us like members of a family are supposed to. She says that when we look in any of our mirrors we should smile so they can show us some of that love.

I used to laugh whenever Mama said this. It wasn't that I didn't believe her, it was just, well… Then I noticed that whenever Mama and Daddy and Marcus and even Jazz look in the mirror, they're smiling. So I figure maybe Mama knows what she's talking about.

After Marcus and Jazz went downstairs, I locked Mama and Daddy's bedroom door. Then I stood in front of the floor mirror and started looking at myself. And smiling.

I saw myself in my new long dress. It was organdy and the color of a rose—my two most favorite things for a dress to be.

I stood there waiting for that mirror to show me some love. Even some like! But all that mirror did was tell me over and over how fat I was.

Why didn't I stay on those stupid diets? Darn, darn, darn, darn, DARN!

I looked in the mirror and saw the future. It would be time for all of Miss Elder's students to be out on the stage taking a bow. Just like we had practiced. Then suddenly my dress would pop open. All the fat I was holding in would start popping out. It might even make a squishy fat sound. Then everybody would start laughing. Maybe even Miss Nickerson!

I stuck my tongue out at the mirror.

You don't love me one bit, you old, long, skinny mirror. I might not ever smile at you again.

20 ✦ *Amanda*

WHEN I WENT to Madelyn's room to ask her about the earrings, I expected her to tell me to get lost. I couldn't believe it when she actually said "yes."

"Are you sure you don't mind?"

"I'm sure, I'm sure. Don't ask me anymore."

I took the earrings out of Madelyn's hand. The ones with the tiny diamonds in the center. They're the most beautiful ones in her jewelry box.

"You're not scared I'll lose them?"

Mother and Dad gave the earrings to Madelyn for her sixteenth birthday. And they're her absolute favorites. She's only worn them about three times herself. She said they were for special, special, special times. She wouldn't even wear them to church.

"Amanda, do you want to wear the earrings for the recital or not?" she said, doing one of her long breaths. She hadn't done one of those for a long time.

"Oh, yes, yes, Madelyn." I closed my fingers over the earrings to make sure they wouldn't fall out of my hand. Then I went over to Madelyn's dresser to see myself while I put them on.

Madelyn still had photos stuck around her mirror, but not as many as before. That was probably because now she had a big picture of Marcus. One of his senior pictures taken for the yearbook, she said. Whatever that was. The big picture was in a frame Madelyn kept on her desk.

I could see Madelyn watching me while I put on the earrings. I was being extra-special careful, but it still looked like something I was doing was bothering her. She looked really sad. Maybe she was sorry she had agreed to let me wear the earrings, and that she couldn't say anything now since I already had them on. Or, maybe...whatever it was, I knew I had to find out.

I turned around so I wouldn't be looking at her through the mirror. "Madelyn," I said, "did you say that I could wear your earrings so I wouldn't say anything to Mother about you and Marcus?"

She got one of those puzzled looks Dad says I get on my face sometimes. She didn't say anything.

I kept on explaining. "Because if you did, you don't have to. I promised I wouldn't tell, and I won't. Honest."

Madelyn just sat there, not saying anything. It was weird.

"And if you said I could wear them because you want me to tell you who won the competition, I really can't. I wish I could, but we all promised that we wouldn't, and I really *can't*..."

I was running out of things to explain, but she just sat there, staring at me. I had to keep talking.

"It's okay, Madelyn. Honest. I wouldn't tell about you and Marcus. Anyway, you were just kissing. Ernestine's not going to tell either. She said she wouldn't, and I believe her. Remember I told you how we actually had fun together at the Jabberwock party? I couldn't believe it. And you'll know who won the contest in a couple of hours. But I'll still understand if you want to take back—"

"Amanda, it's fine if you wear the earrings," Madelyn said, in a kind of faraway voice. "I want you to wear them. Really."

I turned back around and looked real close at myself to see how the earrings looked with my beautiful new dress. They were just like I knew they were going to be. Perfect.

I got up to show Madelyn. I twirled around so my dress would swoosh out. "Look," I said. "How do I look?"

"Oh, Amanda," she said in that faraway voice. "You look …you look beautiful." Then she got up and did something *really* weird. She hugged me.

"I don't care if you won that competition or not. You're going to be the star of the show," she said.

"Thanks, Maawyn," I said.

When I heard the word slipping out, I almost put my hand over my mouth to stop it. I couldn't believe what I was hearing! A name I hadn't called Madelyn since first grade. "Maawyn" was how I had said her name when I first learned how to talk. It was what the whole family had started calling her until I started school.

I thought the sound I heard was Madelyn laughing. But when I pulled out of the hug and looked at her face I saw tears. She was crying!

"Madelyn?"

"It's nothing, Amanda, Really. You look so pretty that... that..." Madelyn's faraway voice was so sad.

All of a sudden I got the weirdest feeling ever. It felt like lots of little bitty people with tiny freezing feet were walking across my back.

"Somethin's wrong, Madelyn. I know it is."

Madelyn started shaking her head "No," but I saw tears.

"Madelyn, I'm getting scared. Please tell me." The freezing feet were moving faster.

Madelyn put her arm around me. Then she started talking in her faraway voice.

"Amanda, I don't want to tell you this now. Especially now, just before the recital. I really, really don't. But since I'm being such a weepy dope, I have to so you'll know what's going on. You'll have to know soon anyway."

Madelyn held my hands with her hands.

"Amanda, Mother and Dad are getting...getting a separation."

I could feel the freezing little feet coming across my shoulders and down into my chest. They were pushing on me and keeping me from thinking about what I should say.

Madelyn was squeezing my hands. She started talking faster. "This isn't really a surprise. We both knew something like this was probably going to happen. It's just that it's something we didn't *want* to happen. But the way things have been lately, I don't know anymore if it should or shouldn't happen. You know what I mean, don't you, Amanda?"

Everything I could feel was pushing on me. Madelyn's hands squeezing mine and the freezing little feet that seemed to be stomping everywhere. I could even feel them near my heart, pushing at my chest.

I was afraid that if I started talking I might begin to cry like Madelyn. But I couldn't cry. My face would get messed up. Mother had put a little rouge on my cheeks, and Madelyn had let me put on some of her pink lipstick. My face would get messed up if I cried. And it just couldn't get messed up. Not now. I had to look perfect for the recital.

"Amanda, are you all right?"

Madelyn had stopped squeezing my hands. She wasn't even holding them anymore. She started rubbing one of her hands across my face. I was afraid she might smear the rouge, so I turned my head away.

I could see my face in the mirror. It looked like something was inside my face, pushing out my cheeks and my eyes. I couldn't feel the tiny feet very much anymore, but everything was still pushing. Then all of a sudden, I knew what it was. I had been holding my breath.

A funny sound flew out of my mouth when I opened it to let my breath out. It sounded like a laugh and a cry at the same time. It was weird, but it had made all the pushing stop.

"I'm okay, Madelyn," I said. I reached for her hand—the one that had been on my face. I didn't want her to think I was mad.

"Are you sure?"

The tiny freezing feet had almost all tiptoed away. I nodded my head "yes" and smiled at Madelyn.

The tears had gone behind Madelyn's eyes. "I know it hurts now, Amanda," she said. "It hurts a lot. But, it might turn out to be a relief. I mean…I bet getting a separation will help Mother and Dad realize how much they used to love each other and how much they want our family to be together."

"Yeah," I said. I still held on to Madelyn's hand, but I didn't say anything. I was keeping my mouth closed tight. I didn't want any more laugh-cry sounds to fly out.

Madelyn's faraway voice was gone. "And whether you won the competition or not, you're gonna be great today," she said.

"Yep, I will," I said.

I took a big breath. A Madelyn-long-deep breath. With the pushing gone, it was easy to breathe again. Especially if I didn't think too much about it.

You'll be fine. You will. Just wait. You'll see.

The little voice I could hear inside sounded like my voice. But I knew it wasn't. In the first place I knew that I wasn't going to be fine. Nothing was. Maybe not ever again.

I wanted to scream out loud and tell the voice to shut up. But I didn't. I just smiled at Madelyn and said that she should hurry up because it was almost time for us to leave.

21 ✑ *Ernestine*

DADDY HELD THE car door open for me just like he does when he helps Mama out of the car. He even held out his hand for me to hold on like he does for her.

"Thanks, Daddy," I said. Hanging on to his hand made it easy for me to hold up my dress and keep it from getting dirty on the bottom.

"Break a leg, baby," Daddy said.

"Daddy!" I practically dropped my dress hearing Daddy tell me to do something so terrible. "Why would you tell me to do that?"

"Yeah, Daddy?" Jazz was leaning out the backseat window. She had heard Daddy, too. "How come you want Ernestine to break her leg."

Mama and Daddy both started laughing. " 'Break a leg' is something you say to someone about to go onstage, sweetheart," Mama said, leaning out her front-seat window. "It's a good luck wish. It means do the *opposite* of breaking your leg.

You know, something wonderful. People in the theater actually think it's *bad* luck to wish someone 'good luck' just before they're going on."

It would be fun not to wish Alicia good luck but to tell her to "break a leg." I was going to ask what other theater things I should know about, but I didn't have any more time. It was almost two-thirty. The time Miss Elder told all of us to be inside the school auditorium, where the recital would be.

"I'll break both legs," I said, and used my free hand to wave good-bye. "See you inside."

It felt strange to be on the stage with the curtains closed. It was like being scared and excited at the same time. But mostly excited. The way people were running back and forth, being kinda nervous but still laughing, I figured everybody felt the same way.

The stage was decorated so pretty! It was lined from one end to the other with flowers. Beautiful flowers of every color you can imagine. All of them were arranged in green pots the color of grass. There were two pianos. Baby grands, like the one in our church. They were in the center of the stage, facing each other, and both of them had their curvy tops propped up. Beside the pianos were posts that looked something like columns with long leafy green things hanging down in front and candleholders on top. Each holder had three white candles. The candles weren't lit yet because that was something Edna had been picked to do right after the curtains opened.

Alicia was the first person I looked for after I stopped looking at the stage. She looked as beautiful as the stage.

She saw me almost the same time I saw her. I waved to her.

"Ernestine!" she said, coming over to where I was. "I've been waiting for you."

Sometimes I have to keep myself from having too much of a dopey grin on my face when I hear Alicia. She has such a sweet voice. A *really* sweet voice. And her smile matches it. Sometimes I want to tell Jazz to take how-to-talk-and-act-sweet lessons from Alicia. Then maybe Jazz wouldn't be so fake.

"Ernestine, you look really nice," Alicia said. It sounded like she meant it, and knowing Alicia, she probably did. I knew that I looked like a round pink blob. But ever since I had looked at myself in Mama's no-love-me mirror and faced the truth, it didn't matter anymore one way or the other.

"Thanks," I said. Then I said something that *was* the truth. "You look beautiful, Alicia."

She did too. Her dress was the same color as peaches, the way they look after you slice them. She had velvet ribbons that matched exactly tied around her hair and her neck. She looked so much like peaches all over that I expected to smell peaches when she leaned over to whisper in my ear. She didn't though. She smelled like always. Lemony.

"Did you see her? Did you see Miss Nickerson?" Alicia's voice was whispery and loud at the same time.

I started looking around. "Where is she?" I said.

Alicia looked around, too. "She was over by the pianos a minute ago," she said. "I guess she went offstage with Miss Elder."

Alicia started walking. She took my hand to pull me along with her. "You've just *got* to see her, Ernestine," she said. "She looks soooooo beautiful. Just like the picture on the poster."

Right away I could imagine what Alicia was talking about. On the posters Miss Elder gave us to put up so everybody could know about the recital, there was a picture of Miss Nickerson. She had on a long, puffed-out dress. The kind ladies used to wear to fancy balls a long time ago. A flower was holding back her hair on one side, and she was sitting at a piano with this big, pretty smile on her face. The words "The Louisiana Lady" were printed below the picture.

"Is she dressed the same way she is in the picture?"

"Just the same," Alicia said. "Only now you can see all the colors, and you can't tell that on the picture."

When we got to the other side of the stage, a puffy white dress with rows of red satin ribbon around it was the first thing I saw. Alicia was right. Miss Nickerson looked even better than she did on the poster. Even better than when I had seen her in church. She looked beautiful.

Miss Elder was beside Miss Nickerson. She had on a regular long dress, not a puffy, old-fashioned kind like Miss Nickerson's, but she looked beautiful, too.

When we got close to them, I held up my hand and waved. I did it without thinking. Then I felt really dumb for doing it.

Miss Elder smiled when I waved at her. "Ernestine!" she said. "You look lovely, dear. That color is beautiful on you."

"Thank you, Miss Elder," I said, smiling back. "Hello, Miss Nickerson.

"Ernestine!" Miss Nickerson came to stand beside me.

"You're the young lady we heard playing the piano in church on Sunday."

I didn't know what to say. I think I was afraid something dumb would pop out. So I just stood there.

Miss Nickerson leaned over to get closer to my face. I could see her eyes so clear. They were dancing!

"You were wonderful, my dear. I was hoping I might have the opportunity to play with you today. I guess I'll just have to look forward to doing that another time."

I practically fell over. I was going to remember this day forever. But I still couldn't think of anything to say.

"You're very talented, my dear," Miss Nickerson said. "Keep practicing, and you'll be the next Philippa Duke Schuyler!" She patted my cheek with her hand, and I could smell lilacs.

"Oh, I will, Miss Nickerson." The words popped out, but I was glad they did. "Thank you," I said as she smiled and walked away.

Suddenly, I wasn't nervous anymore. I didn't feel dumb anymore either. In fact, I was beginning to feel terrific. The feeling stayed even after I saw Amanda standing near the curtains, looking through the space where the two parts of the curtain come together.

The next thing that popped out my mouth *really* surprised me. "Amanda looks nice," I said.

"Um-hmm," Alicia agreed. I knew she meant it, but she sounded kinda strange.

"Is something the matter?" I asked.

"Not with me," Alicia said. "But I think there's something wrong with Amanda."

Alicia didn't say anything else about Amanda and I didn't ask. But when Alicia said she was going to talk to Merry Lou and Carmella, I said I was going to go over and talk to Amanda.

I walked up behind her. "Amanda?" I said.

She turned around to look at me. "What?"

I had been planning to tell her that she looked nice. That's how good I was feeling after talking to Miss Nickerson. Her dress *was* pretty, and Amanda is almost nice-looking. Sometimes. But when she turned around to look at me, she had that same old look on her face. Her evil look. But she also looked sad. Almost like she was ready to cry. Maybe that was what Alicia had been talking about. I decided not to say what I had been planning to say. I decided to kinda kid around with her instead.

"You been lookin' through that curtain practically forever. Are you ever gonna give anybody else a chance?"

"I have *not* been standin' here that long, Ernestine."

"You have so."

"Have not."

I knew inside myself that I was trying to make Amanda feel better. To stop her from thinking about whatever was making her feel sad. Talk about being dumb! I don't know why I would ever try to do that, but for some reason I kept on talking and trying.

"Yes, you have, too. But you might as well keep on now. You've already brought yourself bad luck."

"What are you talkin' about?"

"Remember? Miss Elder told us it would be bad luck to look at the audience through the stage curtain before the show starts."

"If that's true, how come you're so anxious to look through?"

" 'Cause it's *good* luck to have somebody tell you to 'break a leg' before the show starts, and somebody has already said that to me."

Amanda looked at me like she thought I was crazy.

"You think you're gonna have good luck because somebody told you to 'break a leg'? Weird. Really weird."

My good feelings for Amanda were running out.

"Who you callin' weird?"

"I'm not callin' anybody weird. I just said—"

"I heard what you said, Amanda. I've been listenin' to your mouth for months."

"What do you mean, 'months'?"

"Just what I said. Months. You know, like January, February, March…"

"I know what months are, Ernestine. I mean, why are you sayin' you been listening to my mouth for months?"

" 'Cause you always runnin' off at the mouth. You have been ever since that first time I saw you."

"I have not."

"Have so."

"Have not. And anyhow, that first time at Miss Elder's was months and months and months ago, and you probably don't remember back that far any more than I do…"

I should have known it would be useless to try to get into a friendly conversation with Amanda. Why would I think she needed someone to make her feel better? And even if she did, it would never be me. Amanda was going to be Miss Stuck-up forever.

I looked at her standing there beside the curtains. Her long yellow dress with the big sparkly button looked really pretty. Then I saw her eyes. To me they still were sad eyes, but the look on her face was the same old "Amanda, the Evil" look. It made the rest of her look the same way.

Amanda was *really* being dumb. She was letting being evil mess up everything about her. I started to suck my teeth like Jazz does behind Mama's back, and then to just walk away. But something inside kept saying that Amanda's eyes were really sad and that I shouldn't do anything to make her feel worse. So I just waved at her like I had been doing all day. Then I said, "Break a leg, Amanda."

22 ✎ *Amanda*

THE WHOLE TIME we rode to Banneker High School I sat in the backseat next to Madelyn wishing over and over that we would hurry up and get there before Mother said something about Dad's driving and a big argument would start. My wishing must have worked a little. Mother and Dad sat in the front seat like stone statues.

For the first time ever, I was glad to see that raggedy old school building. When Dad pulled up outside the auditorium door, I told everybody I'd see them later and jumped out of the car. I didn't stop to hold up my dress before I ran to the auditorium door even though Mother was yelling at me to be careful. So what if my dress got dirty on the bottom. It wouldn't matter. The whole day wouldn't matter. Not one bit.

To me the stage looked a mess. In the first place, there were so many flowers it was like being at a funeral. I've only been to one funeral, and that was when my great-grandfather died. I didn't know him at all. The only thing I remembered about him was the smell of his funeral. And the stage smelled like his funeral.

Everybody was smiling and walking around and acting busy, like there was a lot to do. But there was nothing to do. Everything was done already. And if anybody did any more to that stage, it was going to collapse.

I finally saw Edna. She was talking to Miss Elder and Miss Nickerson. I didn't feel like saying anything to them yet, so I looked away. I knew Edna would see me sooner or later.

I saw Alicia looking at me. At first I didn't think she was going to speak. But she did finally. She even came over to where I was.

"Amanda, hi," she said.

I said hello to her. After that I couldn't think of anything else to say. But she kept standing there.

"You look nice," she said.

"You do, too," I said.

Alicia did look nice. Her dress was a sorta fruity color, but she looked nice anyway.

"Thanks," she said. "Have you seen the program?"

I shook my head "no."

She had one in her hand. I hadn't even noticed. She handed it to me and moved beside me so we could look at it at the same time.

There was a picture of Miss Elder and Miss Nickerson on the front. Both of them were sitting on a piano bench and smiling. Above the picture was fancy writing that said:

CAMILLE NICKERSON
PRESENTED BY THE ELDER SCHOOL OF MUSIC

I knew Alicia thought all of this was wonderful and wanted me to agree with her. "This is nice," I said. That was all I could think of to say about it.

But that wasn't enough for Alicia. "Wait till you see the back," she said. Her voice was all excited.

I turned the program over and saw all our names. The names of all Miss Elder's students.

"Nice," I said again. There was nothing else to say.

"Don't you like seeing your name on the same program as Miss Nickerson's? She's famous."

I wanted to say, "So what," but I didn't. I remembered how things I said could be used against me. And even though I didn't care anymore, I didn't want the most horrible day of my life to get any more horrible. So I stretched out my lips and hoped they were smiling, and didn't say anything.

Alicia was so different from the way she used to be. In the old days she would have known right away that something was wrong. She would have known even without me telling her. And she wouldn't have asked silly questions either. She would have said something like, "I know something's wrong, Amanda Bear, and I wish you'd tell me. But I'll understand if you don't."

Thinking about how Alicia used to be made me feel worse, and I didn't think I could feel any worse. I was feeling so horrible that I almost…almost started to cry! I just couldn't believe it.

For a long time Alicia didn't say anything. Both of us stood there staring at the program. Then she said, "It's almost time for me to go out front. See you later, Amanda." Then she walked away.

Right after Alicia left, I moved closer to the space between the curtain. I wanted to look out at the audience and see who was there, but mostly I wanted to turn my face away from everybody.

I could see Mother and Dad sitting near the back. Madelyn wasn't with them. She was sitting in the third row with Marcus. It was weird to see how normal Mother and Dad looked. Like everything was fine. Seeing them sitting there like that made me want to yell at them and hug them at the same time.

The audience was filling up. It looked like everybody's family was going to be there. Even brothers and sisters. I saw Ernestine's sister sitting next to their parents. I knew who they were because my godmother had showed them to me that day in church. Jazz was a lot cuter than Ernestine. She wasn't fat either.

Ernestine. Fatso Ernestine. I couldn't believe I was thinking about her. If it wasn't for her, Alicia might still be standing with me by the curtain and talking. We would still probably be best friends. Because of Ernestine I was waiting on the stage by myself while Alicia and Ernestine were getting ready to go out front. They had been chosen to give the welcome to the audience and then to pass out the programs. They'd probably stand together all during the whole program, laughing and talking while I stood backstage by myself. All because of Ernestine. Fatso Ernestine. I hated her!

I began to feel the tiny little feet again. This time they were hot. Burning hot. And they were moving to the front of my face and almost making my eyes water.

"Amanda?"

I couldn't believe it. Ernestine was standing behind me.

I didn't want to turn around, but I did. Finally. "What?" I said.

Ernestine's dress looked like a bunch of droopy, dead flowers. I didn't think she looked so nice, mostly because she's so fat. But she stood there smiling at me like she thought she was beautiful.

I didn't feel like talking to anybody, especially not her. But she stood there anyway, talking to me about looking through the curtain and having bad luck and how she would have good luck and how she had been listening to my mouth for months and some other stuff that didn't make a whole lot of sense.

But there was something else. It was weird. All while I was talking to Ernestine, I didn't think about all the horrible things that were happening to me. I *had* been thinking about them while I was talking to Alicia. Talking to her had even made things worse. But talking to Ernestine was almost making me feel better. It was really weird.

Before Ernestine left to go out front, she said, "Break a leg, Amanda." When she first said something about this being a wish for good luck, I pretended that I didn't know what she was talking about. But I knew all along. I had known ever since the night of the Jabberwock. Edna and I had heard her mom tell that to Dr. Raymond, and we asked about it then. When Ernestine said it to me, I knew she was wishing me good luck.

But that wasn't all. Ernestine looked like she knew something might be wrong. She didn't say anything, but she acted a little bit like she knew.

Like Alicia used to know. Like a friend would know.

Ernestine was gone before I could say anything. Then I saw the two dresses going down the steps. The fruity- and flower-colored dresses. Ernestine and Alicia going out front. Part of me wanted to run after them, but it was almost time for the recital to begin.

I stepped back from the curtain and looked around the bottom of my dress to see if any dirt had gotten on it. There hadn't. I patted my face to make sure it wasn't wet and streaky. It wasn't. Then I went over to the other side of the stage where all the others were lining up. I almost couldn't believe it, but I was sorry Ernestine wasn't there. What was even more weird, I thought about being able to talk to her again after everything was over.

Ernestine & Amanda 🖎

"ERNESTINE?"

"What?"

"Were you mad 'cause you didn't win?"

"Not that *I* didn't win. But I don't think Brenda Wilson should have. She wasn't the best."

"So, who do you think was the *very* best?"

"You."

"*Me?*"

"Are you hard of hearing?"

"I just can't believe it. I mean I can't believe you think *I* was the best."

"How come you always say that?"

"Say what?"

"That you can't believe something. Do you think everybody tells you lies?"

"It's not that. I just can't...I wouldn't think you'd want me to win."

"I didn't say I *wanted* you to win. I said I thought you *should* have won. The piece you played by Miss Nickerson was harder than any of the other pieces. And you played it really good."

"Thanks, Ernestine."

"You're welcome, Amanda."

"I think the piece I played for the contest is the reason I was picked to introduce Miss Nickerson, and that was almost as good as winning. She was super."

"Yep. Especially when she played using nothing but her left hand."

"Yeah. That was fantastic."

"She told me if I kept practicing I would be another Philippa Duke Schuyler."

"Who's that? Somebody else famous?"

"I dunno. I never even heard of her."

"You hadn't heard of Miss Nickerson either, Ernestine. Remember?"

"So?"

"So, just because a person isn't listed in some old book doesn't mean they're not well known."

"Amanda, what are you talkin' about?"

"I said...oh, never mind. Anyhow, since Miss Nickerson asked all of us to bow on the stage with her, maybe now *we're* all famous."

"Yeah. Maybe some day everybody will know the name Ernestine Carroll Harris."

"Well, if they know that, then they're gonna know the name Amanda Nelson Clay, too."

"How you figure that?"

"Just wait. You'll see."